THE HESSON HOUSE

SISTERS OF EDGARTOWN

KATIE WINTERS

CHAPTER ONE

THE MONSTROUS STACK of creative writing papers mocked Olivia from her desk. It stood, formidable as any skyscraper, as she paced back and forth, her phone pinned to her ear. On the other end, Anthony described yet another minor disaster at The Hesson House. The recently renovated boutique hotel located on the coast had just recently held its grand opening, which had been a huge success. It was an old-world mansion that had taken months to restore to its former glory in the wake of her Great Aunt Marcia's death and subsequent will, which had listed Olivia as the new owner of the house. It had been a turbulent time — a whirlwind, to say the least, and Olivia wasn't always sure which direction was up.

"What? He just stormed out of the kitchen?" Olivia lifted a pen to her forehead and clicked at the end of it with her face as frustration brewed.

"Yeah. He threw one of those skillets as he went, too."

"Does he know that each of those skillets cost four hundred dollars?"

Anthony chuckled. "I'm guessing not."

"So, you didn't even need to fire him, I guess?"

"Nope. But we're short-staffed for the night and we're fully booked with even more dinner reservations than normal. Mary told the staff to put out new tables along the waterline. We borrowed a few from the Sunrise Cove."

Olivia had recently hired Mary as a sort of third-in-command, beneath her and Anthony, especially since she'd recently returned to full-time school duties and couldn't be at The Hesson House all hours of the day any longer.

"The Sunrise Cove is always there in a pinch, aren't they?"

"I think they can feel what novices we are. Taking pity on us," Anthony said with a dry laugh.

"We'll take all the pity we can get. What was it we read about the first few years of a hospitality business?"

"One to two years to break even."

"Okay. That's fine. One to two years? That's nothing. It happens in a flash."

"You sound optimistic."

"I'm not. But it's the only way to be, right?" Olivia's smile grew wider. "You put me in a good mood, regardless. What do you say? Let's close the dang thing and move to Hawaii."

"I have a feeling your four best friends would take real issue if I whisked you off to Hawaii like that."

"Oh, I didn't tell you? We're bringing them, too."

Students began to filter in — at first, just a couple stragglers, and then a full burst of them, as though the faucet had been turned all the way up. Olivia blinked up at the sea of sixteen-year-olds who planned to give her about twenty percent of their attention this sixth period as she forced them to discuss a book they probably hadn't bothered to read much of. Could she blame them? The weather was still nice; school had only just begun a few weeks before, so nobody's head was screwed on correctly. Hers certainly wasn't.

"I guess I have to let you go," she said with the slightest of sighs. "Thank you for being there when the skillet was thrown and for all other minor disasters. You know I love you, don't you?"

They'd only just recently started to say the "L" word. It made Olivia's heart swell with happiness.

"I love you, too. Don't let the teenagers bully you into submission."

"I'm sure they'll find a way."

The bell blared with finality. Olivia placed her phone to the right of that monster stack of papers that sat neatly on her desk, cleared her throat, and then faced all twenty-two of her hormonal student-monsters.

"Afternoon, everyone," she said as brightly as she could. "I assume all of you read to chapter four last night in The Great Gatsby?"

There were several side-glances and some grunts. Anxiety permeated through the room like a cloud. Olivia had seen the likes of this time and time again. Finally, the blonde-haired, blue-eyed, doll-like porcelain creature in the back, Samara, shot her arm through the air and said, "I did. I read the chapters."

Her voice wavered. Always, she gave the air of someone on the brink of a meltdown.

"Great. Thank you, Samara. Can you give me a rundown of some of the potential themes you feel Fitzgerald illustrates within these first few chapters?"

Samara's eyes widened with fear. One of the football players, who sat in the corner, chortled and then whispered something to the guy beside him. Samara dropped her eyes to the desk. This class was off to a spectacular start.

"All right, let's outline the themes together." Olivia lifted an erasable marker to the whiteboard and began to scribe as her students drew out their notebooks to take the appropriate notes. "I know it's still early in the year, but I really need you guys to do your reading. You're juniors, which means you only have a year till you start applying for colleges. Many of you will take your SATs this year. It's all about pushing your mind to its limit. It's all about teaching yourself to think in a more profound way. All of you are incredibly capable."

Did she really believe everything she spouted now? She wasn't sure. She'd said all these words time and time again. Students had filtered through her life, year after year, as she had gotten steadily older. Now, at forty-one, she felt a strange shift in how the world dealt with her. She had always been rather shy (unless she stood in front of her students, of course) — but now it seemed that that shyness was a relief to a world that no longer wanted to look at her twice.

AFTER SEVENTH PERIOD'S bell declared the end of yet another school day, Olivia rushed to the teacher's lounge, pulled open her Tupperware, which revealed the packed macaroni and cheese she'd made, and scarfed down half of it. The Pre-Calculus teacher, Janet Maxwell, arched her grey eyebrow toward her and said, "Make sure you chew and swallow your food, young lady."

Olivia tried to laugh, but her mouth was too full. When she swallowed, she said, "I guess I'll have time to eat when I'm dead."

"Keep that dark humor at home, honey," Janet Maxwell told her with an ironic laugh. "We deal with students here. We have enough darkness to handle."

Olivia stretched her long, lean legs out toward her car, which caught the bright reflection of the mid-September sun beautifully. She slid into the front seat and then drove north toward the mansion. She had driven this route so often over the previous months that she hardly remembered the drive. Before she knew it, she shut off the engine and gazed up at the elaborate mansion, its ornate pillars which flanked the porch, and its glowing windows. Gosh, she missed the days when this space had been for her and Anthony, just the two of them — falling in love and mostly covered in plaster and paint. "The good old days," before the "clients" had stormed through the front doors.

Well, of course, they were paying customers. They kept the place afloat. Not that anything felt particularly "afloat" at the moment.

Olivia inspected her makeup in the mirror, added a dash of eyeliner, and then burst out into the open air. Sounds of hotel guests swelled out from the restaurant on the other side of the hotel, where tables spilled out toward the beach. On the left-hand side of the grounds, still, just out of sight, they'd set up a croquet court, and to the left of that, they'd had two tennis courts built. The waiting list for the courts was always about a mile long.

Just as Olivia entered the front door, the pianist seated at the baby grand in the foyer began to tinkle away at another tune. The savoy smells of another glorious lunch rushed out like a wave from the kitchen. Several people continued to sit in the dining area, enjoying mid-afternoon glasses of wine and conversation. Anthony stood at the front desk alongside Mary and an older couple in maybe their sixties, both of whom were dressed immaculately. They looked to be a part of the one percent; even their skin glowed as though they'd drunk some kind of everlasting-life elixir.

"Olivia, so wonderful you're here," Mary beamed in that warm and inviting voice of hers. "Mr. and Mrs. Adams, this is Olivia Hesson. She's the proud owner of The Hesson House. Olivia, Mr. and Mrs. Adams just checked in this afternoon. Apparently, they were good friends with your Great Aunt Marcia."

Olivia extended a hand. "Welcome to The Hesson House. It's so remarkable to meet others who knew my great aunt and what a wonderful woman she was."

"Yes. Your Great Aunt Marcia and I used to vacation in the French Riviera together, in the old days," Mrs. Adams said mischievously. "We got ourselves up to no good."

"I can only imagine." Olivia noted that the woman's eyes traced down the slightest bit, then erupted back up, as though she tried to avoid something. Olivia forced herself not to focus on it.

"Shall I show you to your suite?" Olivia asked.

"They're in the presidential," Mary said knowingly. "But I can take them. I know you have so many things to attend to."

"Nonsense," Olivia said with a wave of her hand. "Come with

me. I assume your luggage has already been brought upstairs?"

"Of course," Mary affirmed. Her eyes told a strange story. Again, Olivia furrowed her brow with confusion, then returned her face to its normal position.

Olivia led Mr. and Mrs. Adams up the winding staircase to the third floor, where the presidential suite took up one entire half of the floor. She told them about each unique antique piece within the suite, about the ornate bed and the claw-footed bathtub and the antique rug, which she'd found in the basement during their renovations.

"Thank you," Mrs. Adams said as Olivia bid them goodbye at the door. "We look forward to our time here."

"Remember to speak to Mary or one of the receptionists about island events over the next few weeks," Olivia told her. "It's only September — not yet winter and the island is still alive and buzzing. Just a tiny bit colder, that's all."

Olivia sauntered back down the staircase. Her hand caressed the smooth wood as she wound down to the main level. When she reached the foyer, Anthony placed his hand at the top of her shoulder, bent his head and whispered, "Come with me."

"Not now, Anthony," Olivia said with a little laugh. "I have a to-do list about a mile long."

"I know. But..." Anthony grimaced. Another couple passed by, headed for the bar area. The pianist switched to another jingle.

"What? You're looking at me like I have three heads."

"It's just that, well, there's no easy way to tell you this." He now spoke quieter than she'd ever heard him.

"What?" she hissed.

"You have melted cheese on your blouse," he said finally. "I only noticed it when you were speaking with the Adams. I'm sorry."

Olivia scrunched her nose tightly. Her eyes traced down toward a big ruffle on her blouse — one she'd bought second-hand from a French fashion collector. Sure enough, a big streak of bright orange, melted cheese blared itself across her breast. How embarrassing.

"Well. I think it's safe to say I'm not juggling this whole high school-slash-hotel schedule well," Olivia said, still looking down at the horrendous display.

Anthony drew his hand over the back of her head and laughed. Slowly, his laughter transformed Olivia's face, and she found space to giggle, too.

"Ah, well. I wondered why Mrs. Adams looked at me like that. Like I was a schlub," Olivia said. "I'll head to the office and clean up. Thank goodness I have extra clothes here."

"I don't know," Mary said from behind the front desk. "I think the cheese stain works for you."

"You think, Mary? Should I keep the look going?"

Mary shrugged. "To be honest, I've seen stranger fashion trends. And at least this could become a snack later."

Anthony cackled as Olivia rolled her eyes and headed back to her office. "I swear. If you two don't tell me the next time I have any kind of food on my blouse in front of high-paying guests, you're both fired!"

"Good! Fire us! See if you can do this by yourself!" Mary bantered brightly.

Olivia whipped around and placed her palms together. "Come on, Mary. You know I worship the ground you walk on. Keep up the good work, you two! It's crunch time. It's always crunch time."

CHAPTER TWO

"CHELSEA! HEY!" The words blurted out from the steaming kitchen as Chelsea rushed past, en route to her ten-top by the window. She yanked herself around to find her boss, Marty, in the doorway, his eyes stern. Chelsea's heart burst wildly. Had she done something wrong?

"What's up?"

"We need you to take the three-top by the bar," he told her.

"Ugh, I'm so swamped right now," Chelsea groaned. She adjusted the tray on her palm and staggered the slightest bit. The drinks on the tray sloshed dangerously, but they remained within the confines of their glasses. Thank goodness.

"Everyone's swamped, but you told me you need the money," Marty told her.

Chelsea swallowed the lump in her throat. "All right. Yeah. I'll take 'em."

"Good girl."

Chelsea resented when he called her that. She grumbled to herself as she swept toward the window with the heavy tray. Her bicep bulged beneath as she stretched out the tray onto the edge of one end of the table and greeted the party with a bright smile. Every move she made, every word she spewed would all add up to the tip they inevitably gave at the end of their "high-end, experiential" dinner. This place in Manhattan, Tiny Tim's, had nothing at all to do with the diner she'd spent the previous several years serving at. It was the big leagues and it made her sick.

"Big night tonight!" one of the men at the table hollered to her. He was the head of the large family. Clearly, the one who would pay the bill at the end, and Chelsea forced a huge all-American girl smile for him.

"Yeah! What are you celebrating tonight?"

"We've got our daughter here going to NYU," the man said as he beamed at the girl beside him proudly. "She started a few weeks ago and already turned in an A paper."

"Dad..." The girl's cheeks flushed crimson with annoyance. "You don't have to tell every person we run into about the paper."

"Hey, a Dad can brag. I'm just proud of our girl, is all," the man returned.

"I think it's great you celebrate things like that," Chelsea said.

"I'm sure your father does the same!" the man returned.

Chelsea passively agreed, then headed off to greet that three-top near the bar. Her legs were quick as lightning, muscular and trained from years of waitressing. She felt herself recommending various cocktails — always the most expensive ones, of course, and ensuring that each guest was greeted warmly. By the time she returned to the kitchen, her five-top's dinner was served, and she had to hustle back out and dot the finely plated salmons, steaks, and portions of pasta out across the white tablecloth without skipping a beat.

As her legs hustled her back to the kitchen, the man's words rolled around her mind again. "I'm sure your father does the same." Well, no. He didn't. Tyler had left Martha's Vineyard when Chelsea had been thirteen years old and in the wake of that, he'd gone off, started a new life in Boston, and subsequently forgotten about her.

Now, his girlfriend was pregnant. Chelsea was poised to be a big sister for the first time in her life, at the idiotic age of nineteen. What kind of relationship would that be? She would be twenty-nine when the girl was ten. Thirty-nine when the girl was twenty. She pictured herself at forty, taking out this non-existent girl for her first legal drink. "This is my big sister," the girl would say and Chelsea would grin that forty-year-old grin and feel just about as stupid as ever. "And this is the girl my father decided to raise properly," she would probably think.

Or maybe she wouldn't. Maybe she would love that girl to bits. Maybe she would bring color and energy to her life in ways she couldn't comprehend. But optimism couldn't fully find her, not then. Not when she was so busy at Tiny Tim's and very, very unsure if she would find her way to closing time.

Toward eleven-thirty at night, Chelsea managed to find a two-minute window to pee. This was a rare thing indeed. She had trained herself like a dog to wait to head to the restroom until the last possible moment. Once in the bathroom, she lifted her phone for the first time and discovered three text messages from the outside world. When Tiny Tim's got too frantic, she sometimes felt that the rest of Manhattan, of New York, of the greater United States of America, didn't exist at all. All there was were new food tickets, hungry guests, and an angry boss who frequently gave her a once over with his eyes that made her spine shiver.

Two of the texts were from Xavier, her boyfriend.

XAVIER: I'll be out late tonight. I told Gavin I'd help him with his app.

XAVIER: I hope it's not as wild tonight at TTs, but I know that's wishful thinking. And I know we need the money. Just know that I love you, okay?

The next text was from her mother.

MOM: Today, I greeted a super ritzy couple with melted cheese on my shirt. I hope your day is better than mine. Love you! :)

Chelsea giggled inwardly. For reasons she couldn't fully comprehend, she had begun to think of the island and her mother much differently since her departure. For years, all she had wanted was to run out of that place and build a life of her own. Now that she and Xavier lived in their dank Brooklyn apartment, dealt with a bad landlord, and had rough jobs of their own, she wasn't fully sure why she had wanted to trade in the glittering waters, bright blue skies and white sandy beaches. She'd had a reason, hadn't she?

After she closed out her final table for the night, Chelsea counted up her tips — a whopping 377 dollars in five hours, which wasn't bad anywhere else, but this was New York City, and there was rent to pay. Still, it made her laugh to remember her piddling tips at the diner. Usually, she left the place with fifty bucks, tops.

When she had been sixteen, fifty bucks had felt like one million dollars, give or take.

Chelsea took the subway home. It was just past one in the morning, but in the city that never sleeps, that mattered very little in terms of how busy the train was. She stood and gripped the handle overhead as the train jerked her to and fro. A woman at the far end of the train wore a bright pink boa and ticked her finger to the left and right as though she wanted to warn Chelsea of something.

Chelsea was sometimes overjoyed with the city. This was true. She remembered those first few days with Xavier before either of them had nabbed their jobs when they'd explored as much of the city as possible, hungry for every nook and cranny and every potential story. They were still too young to check out the various bars, unfortunately, but they spent their money at coffee shops and watched old New Yorkers as they met one another and chatted over cigarettes outside.

"Maybe that will be us one day," Chelsea had said to Xavier.

"Smokers?"

"No! No. Just — we'll have so many stories of being in the city for so long. We'll feel like this place really belongs to us."

Xavier had considered this. After a long sip of coffee, he had replied, "I think I want that. I wonder what we'll think of the Vineyard after being away for so long."

"Maybe it will feel like just a distant dream of the past."

Chelsea got off the train and walked with her hands shoved into her pockets back toward their apartment in Brooklyn. The streets were relatively busy; people rushed in and out of bars and hollered for their friends. Girls were dressed in incredible ways — long legs swept down toward their high heels, and tight dresses hugged gorgeous curves. Chelsea wondered if she would one day count herself among them. Maybe she, too, would go to NYU or another school in the city if she ever got up the courage to apply. Her mother certainly wanted that for her. Her SAT scores had been pretty good, in fact. Chelsea just hadn't known what to do with them.

When Chelsea reached her apartment building, she saw a scary sight: a dark figure that looked like a middle-aged man, who sat on the stoop. She stopped about ten feet away and took in the full view of him. He had his arms wrapped around his knees, and his head was bent forward. He eased back and forth like a crying child. It was clear he'd been drinking. She could practically smell the alcohol coming off of him. But when he lifted his head, as though he sensed her presence, she recognized him all the more.

It was her father. It was Tyler.

"Dad?" Shock wasn't a strong enough word for it. She gaped at him — at the man who had taught her how to ride a bicycle and helped her with her arithmetic homework. It had to be him, but it was as though this was the beginning of a horrible nightmare.

Tyler tried to stand, but his knees clacked together and he collapsed on the stoop again. Chelsea hustled up to him and extended a hand. It was a funny thing. Only a moment before, she had assumed he was a predator, someone with the potential to hurt her. Now, his hand slid into hers and she guided him into the building and then up two sets of stairs, into her apartment. She couldn't ask questions on the street.

Once inside, Tyler grumbled and mumbled mostly to himself. He swatted at his coat and then collapsed at the edge of the couch, a second-hand thing she and Tyler had found at the far end of the block, deposited by someone who had moved on with his life.

Chelsea acted quickly. She was still in waitress mode. She filled a large glass of water and passed it to her father and instructed him to drink it. He took a slight sip and then coughed. She crossed her arms over her chest and wondered what the heck to do next.

"Dad, what are you doing here?" she asked, hands-on-hips clearly annoyed.

Tyler swiped a hand over his mouth. He looked at her with big, gaping eyes — eyes that gave her no conclusion.

"Dad, why aren't you in Boston?"

He shook his head somberly. It was clear he didn't know at that moment.

Chelsea returned to the kitchen counter. Her hands shook as she lifted her phone and texted Xavier.

CHELSEA: You need to get home. Right now.

CHELSEA: My dad is here for some reason. He's wasted. I've never seen him like this.

CHELSEA: I'm scared.

Almost immediately, Xavier texted back.

XAVIER: Leaving now.

XAVIER: Call the cops if you need to.

CHELSEA: No! He's my dad.

Chelsea spun around again to find that her father had drawn his legs up onto the couch. He still wore his shoes. A snore slipped out from his throat as he sank into darkness. His hair was strewn out across the couch pillow. She wasn't sure why her heart swelled with love for him then. He was the first sign of home she had seen in weeks.

Slowly and methodically, Chelsea untied his shoelaces and placed his shoes near the door, alongside her and Xavier's. She then placed a quilt over his legs and adjusted it over his chest. She stood near the kitchen, shivering until Xavier arrived home about twenty minutes later. When he saw her, she fell into his arms and wept. It had been a hell of a night.

CHAPTER THREE

OLIVIA SHIFTED GENTLY IN BED. Her soft sheets swept across her legs and curled over her stomach, and she dug her head deeper into her pillow and prayed that the alarm would go off to haunt some other creature. Beside her, Anthony slept on. He had his back turned to her, that broad, muscular back of his, and with every breath, he seemed to grow three times the size of his normal size before a slight snore sent him back again. She pressed a hand against his back tenderly as her heart stirred with love. Yet again, she found herself counting her blessings. She hadn't done that enough when Tyler had been around. She hadn't forced herself to appreciate every single, silly day, whether it was good or bad. She wouldn't make that same mistake again.

She rose a few minutes before her alarm, shut it off, and padded into the kitchen to brew a pot of coffee. There was a chill to the September morning, and she reached for an old flannel in the front closet and wrapped herself up like a burrito. It was six-fifteen already, and she faced another frantic day which would result in an eight-hour workday at the high school, followed by six or seven hours working at The Hesson House.

She poured herself a cup of black coffee, considered milk and then thought better of it. She then grabbed her phone from the charger. What happened next was like a bomb going off.

Chelsea had texted her at around two in the morning, then two-thirty, then three, then three-thirty. Olivia felt as though there was a storm in the far distance, headed her way.

CHELSEA: I don't know how to tell you this, but Dad appeared at my door tonight. Late. After my shift.

CHELSEA: He was so drunk. I thought he was just some crazy guy on the street, and then bam, it was Dad, and I brought him in and he passed out on the couch.

CHELSEA: Xavier came home right away, and we're okay, but I have absolutely no idea what to do.

CHELSEA: I don't know. I don't know. Probably, it's all fine. Maybe he just came to visit.

Olivia's heart pattered dangerously. This sort of behavior was bizarre, even for Tyler. No, she didn't know a great deal about Tyler's life these days — just that his girlfriend, Casey, was about to give birth. And probably that had brought up a whole lot of chaos for him. Olivia had known Tyler since their high school days; it wasn't hard to figure out what was going on with him, even from the island.

Still, showing up drunk to his adult daughter's apartment in Brooklyn was a low blow. Maybe the lowest of all the lows.

Immediately, Olivia called Chelsea on her cell. It rang twice before Chelsea answered groggily.

"Mom?"

"Hi, honey." Olivia's speech felt handicapped. "I just got your messages."

Chelsea buzzed her lips. Olivia could practically see her, how she probably rubbed her eyes and then rolled them back in early morning annoyance. How often she had seen that grouchy version of Chelsea; now, she missed every version of her.

"Yeah. Sorry. I kind of went off the rails last night."

"Understandable. Gosh, I didn't expect this."

"Neither did I." Chelsea paused for a moment and then muttered something off to the side, probably to Tyler. Olivia felt a pang of sorrow and anxiety as though she had interrupted her daughter during a private moment. "Anyway, Xav says he's still conked out on the couch."

"Maybe you should wake him up? Demand answers?"

"I don't know." Chelsea was silent for a moment.

Olivia had to fight her every instinct to demand Chelsea to put her on the phone with Tyler. She remembered the volatile fights they'd had in the years before Tyler's departure to Boston. She could rekindle that anger. She could find the words.

"I'm sure when he wakes up, he'll explain everything," Chelsea told her then.

Olivia's heart dropped. This was typical Chelsea: always on her father's side. The door creaked from the bedroom, and Anthony stepped out, rubbing the top of his head. He furrowed his brow when his eyes met Olivia's. She probably looked pale as a ghost.

"What's wrong?" he mouthed.

"I can call everything off today," Olivia said suddenly. "I can be in Brooklyn in just a few hours."

"Don't be ridiculous, Mom." Now, Chelsea pulled out her obstinate, teenage voice — the one that very pointedly put Olivia in her place.

Olivia knew better than to blow on the flames. "You'll tell me when you know more, right?"

"Of course," Chelsea returned. "I'm going to try to get more sleep. I have a long shift tonight and a lot to deal with. The city is a lot, Mom."

"I know, honey." Olivia's heart shattered. "I love you."

"I love you, too."

At least she'd said it. At least she still felt that way. At least they still had their mother-daughter bond, even after Chelsea had run off the island to "find herself" in the city. Olivia placed her phone on the counter as her shoulders shook. Anthony stepped up behind her and placed a hand on her shoulder to steady her.

Anthony entered the room. "What's going on? What happened?"

"Tyler is there, apparently." Olivia placed her hands over her eyes and tried to dismiss all of this as just a nightmare. "He showed up drunk and then he just passed out on her couch."

"My God."

"I know. It's bad, even for him. And his girlfriend is about to have their baby. I mean, is he going to go break up another family?"

Olivia had the sense that Anthony had a whole lot of things to say about this but instead decided to keep his lips sealed. It did nobody any good for the new boyfriend to be talking smack about her ex-husband. Olivia was grateful for this. Plus, Anthony knew the intricacies of exes. His wife had cheated on him with his best friend; he had left Providence, thinking that he would never see his daughter again. In the wake of that, he and his daughter had restored their relationship to what it had been previously, and she'd even come to the island frequently over the summer. Olivia had really taken to the girl. The word "stepmother" no longer freaked her out so much. Not that Anthony was on the verge of any kind of proposal.

"Poor Chelsea," is what Anthony said instead.

"That's what I keep coming back to, too," Olivia admitted. "She didn't ask for any of this. Tyler left her and now he's come back to use her as some kind of crutch."

"Why don't you call in a sick day today? You have too much on your plate right now and it would do you some good to focus. We could hang out at the hotel. Wait for more info. And, you know, put out any more hotel fires while we're at it."

"I don't know. I already feel like I'm not giving those kids my full attention," Olivia said. "I should go. It'll take my mind off of things to talk about books and writing all day."

In the shower, Olivia found herself lost in thought as the razor-sharp jolts of hot water ran over her back. She scrubbed her scalp, washed her body, and then stepped into the steam of the bathroom. The mirror was nothing but fog. In a rush, she wrapped the towel around her body and headed for her closet, where she selected a pair of slacks and another blouse.

Anthony had turned on the television in the living room. It

blared with news of a baseball game. The sound was like a drone, and it calmed Olivia's thoughts. She'd always marveled that men took such solace in sports. "Don't you know there are books in the world?" she'd always wanted to ask Tyler. But just then, the fact that some guys got paid to throw a tiny white ball around on a field gave her a soft, tender feeling. It was easy, but there were rules.

Olivia decided to stop by the Frosted Delights Bakery en route to school that morning. She waited behind two couples, both of whom seemed to be Martha's Vineyard tourists. They took just about forever to decide what flavor of donut they wanted. Olivia shifted her weight and crossed and uncrossed her arms. Really? On today of all days?

Finally, she stepped up to find Jennifer, the red-headed beauty, beaming at her from the other side of the counter. Jennifer tucked a long strand of hair behind her ear and grinned broadly.

"And what can I do for you, stranger?"

Olivia couldn't help it. Jennifer's smile was infectious. She returned it, then immediately burst into tears. Why couldn't she control her emotions? Jennifer rushed around the counter and flung her arms around her, then hurried her into the back and sat her at the very table she and the other girls had congregated around during their teenage years, eating far too many snacks and gossiping about boys. It all seemed like somebody else's life.

Olivia explained what had happened in Brooklyn the night before while Jennifer placed a maple donut on a plate and listened intently.

"That Tyler. He always knows how to get himself into trouble," she said.

"True. I know. What did I ever see in him? All those years, hung up on him in high school…"

"Come on. We've all loved people we shouldn't have," Jennifer said.

"Um, maybe most people can say that, but you can't," Olivia returned. "Joel was and still is pretty perfect. And now Derek…"

Jennifer shrugged. "Yeah, but look at everyone else. Mila just went on a date with a stalker. Amelia's giving birth to a really mean guy's baby. Camilla's husband is about a million red flags all tied up into one man, but she still loves him to pieces."

"I was kind of split about whether or not they should have gotten back together, to be honest," Olivia said quietly.

"She seems happy, really happy. That's all that matters, right?"

Olivia nodded. Jennifer poured her a cup of coffee, which she sipped gently.

"What can I do for you today?" Jennifer asked. "Anything?"

"Maybe you could stop time for a minute, so I could get some more sleep?"

"I'll figure out time travel for the both of us," Jennifer offered. "I've been burning the candle at both ends all year long. And goodness me, that Katama Lodge always needs me for one social media disaster after another."

Olivia chuckled. "That whole incident with that celebrity Helen Skarsgaard was quite a show."

"Yeah. I'm sure it was a show from here. From a PR standpoint, it was initially a disaster," Jennifer said as she bugged her eyes out.

Olivia stood at the head of her class as the eight a.m. bells blared overhead. She was light-headed and woozy. She wished she would have brushed her teeth after that donut. She addressed her fourteen and fifteen-year-old freshmen with wet eyes, which threatened to spill tears.

"Who wants to read the next act in Romeo and Juliet?" she asked. "I need a Romeo and a Juliet."

Nobody raised his or her hand. This was classic; a war between teacher and students. Finally, Olivia randomly pointed to a girl and a boy, both good-looking. This was a bit like playing with fire. Guaranteed, their hormones were pent up. After a few "thous" and "shalls," they could very well fall in love, end up at prom together, and then wind up in the midst of a messy divorce twenty years down the road.

This was a poisonous thought.

The girl's voice began meekly as she recited Juliet's words:

"Wilt thou be gone? It is not yet near day. It was the nightingale, and not the lark, that pierc'ed the fearful hollow of thine ear..."

And in response, the Romeo of the group said, in a voice that wavered between deep and high, due to hormones, *"It was the lark, the herald of the morn, no nightingale. Look, love, what envious streaks do lace the severing clouds in yonder east... I must be gone and live, or stay and die."*

The class erupted with laughter. Olivia arched a brow and said, "You know, Romeo and Juliet were about your age in this play." This shut them up again. Olivia instructed the two of them to continue their reading. Meanwhile, she reached back and stole a quick glance at her phone to see if Chelsea had sent any messages. Still nothing.

CHAPTER FOUR

CHELSEA STOOD AGAIN at the kitchen counter and gripped a mug of coffee. Her father remained in the exact same position he had fallen asleep in, as though, in his drunken state, his muscles were too depleted for any tossing or turning. As she sipped the hot liquid, Xavier stepped past her, clearly disgruntled. He swept a backpack over his shoulder then turned to follow Chelsea's gaze toward the middle-aged man on the couch.

"You going to wake him up?"

"Yeah, I will. After you leave."

Xavier gave her a dark look. Always, he was a bit too protective — something Chelsea had previously really liked about him. They had only kindled their romance after she'd fallen through that stupid hole in the back of The Hesson House and broken her leg. He hadn't left her side for months, it seemed like. Now, he struggled to leave her side, and Chelsea found herself aching for breathing space.

"I can wait for you to wake him up. We can press him for info together."

"We aren't good cop, bad cop," Chelsea told him. "I'm his daughter. I've known him my entire life. I think I can handle this." Even as she said it, a wave of doubt crashed against her stomach. She sipped her coffee and forced herself to make heavy eye contact with Xavier, with the kind of expression that meant business.

"Okay." Xavier dropped down and kissed her gently on the lips. "I love you, Chels. Call me if you need anything."

"I will. I love you, too."

When the door clicked closed, Tyler jumped the slightest bit into consciousness. He coughed twice, making his eyelids flutter open slightly and then close again. He exhaled into himself and seemed to weave his way back to sleep. Chelsea wouldn't have it.

"Dad. Dad?" Her voice grew louder, more demanding. She stepped up to the couch as a wave of his smell — a mix of body odor and alcohol, crashed over her. "Dad! I need you to get up. Now!"

She sounded like her mother before school. She detested it.

Tyler sensed that "Olivia" vibe, as well, because he finally did draw back those eyes and blink up at her. Chelsea's nostrils flared. She did not need this right now.

"Chels. Hi."

Chelsea's eyes threatened to spill over tears, but she wouldn't let them.

"Dad, what are you doing in Brooklyn?"

Tyler brought his hands up to his face and rubbed his eyes. Chelsea had always loved his hands. They were big and capable, the kinds that could fix her dollhouse or her bicycle or the car in the dead of winter.

"Do you mind if I take a shower?" he finally asked. "It would clear my head."

Chelsea nodded before she stepped into the bedroom to find the only clean towel there on the hanging shelf they'd bought from Target for thirteen bucks. She tossed it to her father, who caught it in mid-air. Apparently, his hangover didn't affect his reflexes.

"There's shampoo and soap in the shower," she told him.

Tyler swept a hand over his five o'clock shadow. "Does Xavier have any other razors?"

Chelsea felt awkward handing her father one of the dollar brand razors, which Xavier purchased and used infrequently. She couldn't begin to tell her father just how poor they were. Probably, he could sense it off the old couch he slept on and the general air of the place, as though it could produce a rat infestation out of thin air. But he wasn't exactly in the position to judge, was he?

While Tyler was in the shower, Xavier texted Chelsea to check-in. She ignored it. She wanted to speak with her father first before she reported back. In the bedroom, she changed into jeans and a t-shirt and then changed into a dress and her second-hand leather jacket, which her mother had purchased for her for Christmas the previous year. If there was one thing Olivia had, it was style sense. She and all her best friends had it, and it had been engrained in Chelsea from an early age: *if you want to feel your best, you have to look as best as you can.*

Xavier was a bit smaller than Tyler, which made the clothing situation problematic. Chelsea grabbed a college sweatshirt from Xavier's collection and tossed it his way as he sat in just his jeans on the couch.

"This is fine," Tyler said. "I'll make it work."

But as Chelsea and Tyler walked down the streets of Brooklyn on this beautiful morning in mid-September, Chelsea couldn't help but feel that she walked alongside an oversized fraternity brother. He looked completely out of place in that sweatshirt, with his hair disheveled from drying post-shower. They still hadn't said many words to one another, and Tyler had expressed that he'd never been this hungover in his life.

"It's a cumulative hangover," he explained. "I've been drinking for a few days."

Chelsea led him to a nearby greasy-spoon diner. It had a few elements of the diner she so loved back in Edgartown, with the added spin of classic New Yorker types. There was even a juke box in the corner.

They sat at a corner booth and ordered breakfast sandwiches with egg, bacon and cheese.

"Keep the coffee coming," Tyler told the waitress as she sped away from the table.

Chelsea wanted to tell Tyler not to order the waitress around like that, but she held her tongue. What did he know about the service industry? Besides, he didn't fully know what his tone was like just then. He was a mess.

After their coffee came, Chelsea wrapped her hand around her mug and peered into her father's exhausted eyes.

"All right, Dad. I think it's time to fess up." She tried to say it in a joking manner, but it came out rather hard.

Tyler swallowed a sip of coffee and then turned his eyes to the table. "I can't begin to understand what it must have felt like to find me like that last night. I hardly remember it. I'm so sorry. Really, I am."

The apology was almost enough. Chelsea nodded. "I admit that it was scary finding my dad like that."

"I won't do that to you again. I promise," he lamented.

Chelsea wanted so badly to believe him that she just decided to go ahead and do it. She sipped her coffee again, then asked, "So, what happened?"

"You know. I'm not as strong as I seem, all the time," Tyler began.

"I don't think anyone is."

"Maybe. I don't know. I've made so many mistakes over the years, Chels. Leaving you and your mom, I mean, I don't know if I'll ever fully forgive myself for that. Your mother and I weren't really in love anymore. Maybe we never were, I don't know. We got off to a rocky start and it just continued to spiral out of control from then on out."

"I know that. I heard you up fighting night after night, after all."

"Sure. You were there for all of it. I know." Tyler squeezed his eyes shut as though a pang of a headache had just struck him. "You know that Casey is about to give birth in just a few weeks."

"I'm very well aware of that."

"Well. Then, you probably figured already, because you're a smart cookie like your mom, that I'm here because I'm freaked out about it. And Casey and I have started to fight like cats and dogs. Everything she does enrages me and everything I do makes her incredibly sad. We don't mix anymore and to be honest, my drinking has taken a real turn."

Chelsea wanted to say something sarcastic like, *you don't say?* But she held it in.

"And so, I came back drunk the other night, and Casey told me

I wasn't allowed in. She had some guy there with her, this big guy, and he blocked the door. He threatened to call the police if I did anything. I asked him what the hell he could tell the police since this was my house. But he just stood there and overpowered me and I felt so, so small, stupid and drunk, Chels. And before I knew it, I'd checked into a hotel and ordered myself a bottle of whiskey. I drank that. And called Casey's voicemail and screamed at her a few times. I don't know if she heard them. I don't even know what I said."

"Jesus, Dad." Chelsea had to admit, this was a side of her father she didn't want to see. None of this should be put on her shoulders. She was the daughter, not his counselor. There was such darkness to this man; something she'd been able to pretend didn't exist beforehand.

"Anyway, I suddenly found myself headed here. I checked out of the hotel and got on a bus and then suddenly, I was in Brooklyn. I knew where you lived because you'd sent me an email with your address in it. There I was, like an idiot, waiting for you to come home. And around then, I guess, I blacked out."

Chelsea grimaced at the sight before her. Her father sat there looking like a very broken man. The waitress arrived with their breakfast sandwiches and refilled their coffees with a quick swoop of the spouted pot. The only thing Chelsea could think to do now was ask questions.

"Have you talked to Casey at all since you saw her at your house?"

"No. She hasn't texted me or returned any of my calls," Tyler replied.

"Do you think there's a way you could fix things with her?"

Tyler shrugged and then bristled the slightest bit. "I honestly don't know. I have no idea what to do. And right now, I want to eat this breakfast sandwich. Okay?"

Chelsea hated when her father got like this. She crossed her arms over her chest and turned her head as her father tore into his sandwich. The egg cracked, and the yolk of it smeared across the plate beneath. There had to be some kind of poem written about such an incident: the moment you realized you had more power over your life than your father, who was always meant to "take care" of you.

Tyler placed his sandwich back on his plate and swiped the napkin over his fingers. "Anyway, I was wondering if I could sleep on your couch for a few days, just until I decide what to do next."

Throughout Chelsea's teenage years, all she had wanted was her father to return home. She'd called him all the time and begged him to come home. He had always told her he couldn't but that he would visit soon. Now, she had him there and the roles were reversed. Life was a funny thing.

"Sure, but only for a few days," Chelsea said. "Our place is a shoebox."

"We'll make do," Tyler said with a crooked grin.

A long time ago, Olivia had tried to explain to Chelsea why she'd fallen in love with Tyler in the first place. *"He was so charming, endlessly charming. I had always felt so invisible until he looked at me and made me feel whole again. But Chelsea, I'm telling you. Never be like me. You're whole in your own right. Don't leave it to a man to tell you what you are or what you're not. It took me a long, long time to learn that. But you're stronger than me."*

Apparently, Chelsea wasn't so different because she melted like butter at her father's request. "I'll just text Xavier to tell him what's happening," she said, praying Xavier wouldn't be too upset.

Guess what, babe? We're getting a new roommate. My dad!

CHAPTER FIVE

OLIVIA SAT in the teacher's lounge with her microwave lasagna and picked at it without interest. She had sent Chelsea four texts that morning, prying her for information. Chelsea had read all of them and hadn't bothered to respond. Olivia's mind burned with fear. What the heck had happened next?

Janet Maxwell sat alongside her at the circular table and unwrapped her tuna fish sandwich. The smell was rancid. "You doing okay, Olivia?"

"Oh, yes. I'm fine. I have a mountain of papers to grade, as usual, but no complaints otherwise." This was a huge lie. "What about you?"

Janet countered that she was up to her ears in student complaints. "I get it. Nobody wants to learn math. But it's not like I'm the one who invented the SAT."

"Yes, of course. We're just a part of the system. We didn't invent it."

Janet chewed contemplatively. After a pause, she asked, "And how is Chelsea holding up in Brooklyn? Always such a bright girl."

"She's doing well," Olivia returned. "She and Xavier seem very happy. She sends me a lot of photos and talks like she'll be a full-fledged New Yorker."

"She'll always be an islander," Janet returned, an attempt to soothe her. "Don't you worry about that. And who knows? She might get this whole city thing out of her system and decide to come on home. Isn't that what these kids always learn when they leave? That they needed their moms a whole lot more than they thought."

Olivia's phone buzzed. She tore her eyes toward it, praying for contact from Chelsea. But instead, it was Anthony.

"Hey. What's up?"

Anthony's voice was ragged. "I don't know how to tell you this."

Another disaster. "Go on."

"Mr. Adams had a heart attack in the middle of lunch," Anthony continued. "Everyone's panicked. The mood at the hotel is very strange. The ambulance just left."

"Oh, God." Olivia tore from her chair so fast that it fell back behind her. "I'll be right there."

"Good. Mary and I have a whole lot of panicked guests on our hands. We're not sure how to move forward."

Olivia re-wrapped her lasagna, which was almost completely untouched, and rushed to the hallway. Janet hollered as she went: "I hope you're all right!" But Olivia didn't pause to answer. She reached the office a few seconds later and told the receptionist that she needed a sub for the remainder of her classes for the day. This wasn't the first time of the year she'd done this, and the receptionist let out a huff.

"You sure you can do both?" she asked as she drew up the list of subs. "That hotel is really taking up a lot of your time."

"It's an emergency," Olivia countered. She then rushed back to her classroom, grabbed her autumn jacket, and jangled her keys nervously all the way back to her car, passing several students in the hall on the way. The Great Gatsby would have to wait for another day. The sub would just do what she always did — play a movie and let the kids goof off for fifty minutes. Olivia couldn't worry about that right now.

Olivia rushed to The Hesson House, parked out front, and ran up the porch steps and into the foyer. Just as the door creaked open, she checked her blouse for any sign of melted cheese or sauce. This time, she was in the clear.

Mary stood at the front desk speaking with a number of guests. Two of them were clearly upset, crying.

"We'll let you know as soon as we know more," Mary tried to console them.

Olivia stepped up to the plate with a vibrant smile. "Hello, everyone."

Immediately, the guests breathed a welcome sigh of relief at the sight of the owner.

"He just fell over," a middle-aged woman in a Ralph Lauren cardigan breathed.

"That's awful. We have some of the best doctors on the east coast on staff at the hospital," Olivia assured her. "And in the meantime, why don't all of you head to the outdoor bar? Drinks are comped for the afternoon, along with a selection of tapas and snacks. We want you to continue to enjoy yourselves here."

The guests glanced at one another with the slightest bit of doubt. One of the men shifted his head back and said, "I wouldn't mind a negroni, actually."

"Yes. Our bartender is an excellent mixologist," Olivia assured him, her voice soothing.

The man drew his fingers over his wife's hand and led her back through the dining room and out into the open air. The other guests followed behind. Olivia's eyes found Mary's, as Mary shuddered. All the color drained from her cheeks.

"It wasn't good. He was passed out cold on the ground," Mary tried to explain under her breath. "And Mrs. Adams was totally despondent, then crying, and it just broke everyone's heart at once."

"Did the EMT workers say anything? Anything to make you think one way or the other..."

Mary shook her head. "It didn't look good."

"Oh, God. That's not good." Olivia's heart stirred with sorrow. She'd only just met the Adams couple. They were polite and considerate and beautiful — and they held within them memories of her Great Aunt Marcia, which meant the world to her. It felt like a terribly bad sign that this had happened.

"Let's make sure all the other guests know about the free drinks and snacks," Olivia said. "I want this place to have a healthy ecosystem and positive energy flowing throughout. Let's all try to move past this traumatic event."

Olivia headed down the hallway toward her office. As she passed the piano, the pianist sat at the edge of the stool, and she instructed her to play "upbeat" tunes, "nothing too dark, please!"

The pianist nodded and began to play "Fly Me To The Moon." Olivia hummed to herself as she continued back into the private, staff-only area of the large mansion. All the while, she considered something she hadn't in all the months since she and Anthony had begun to build up the place into this boutique hotel.

The thing about hotels was this: they carried within them countless memories, guests passing through en route to the next level of their journey. But nobody ever knew when their journey was meant to end. There wouldn't only be positive and beautiful days at The Hesson House. There would be dark ones as well and they would certainly color Olivia's mindset if she allowed them to.

Anthony sat at his desk, which sat opposite to Olivia's in the big office space they'd selected for themselves. His face was tremendously pale and slightly green. Olivia rushed for him and threw her arms around him.

"Are you okay?"

"I was right by him," Anthony murmured. "We'd just been talking about having a round of tennis later today. Then, he was on the ground."

"Gosh. I'm so sorry, Anthony." Olivia drew her fingers through his hair as her heart drummed with sorrow. "And Mrs. Adams went with him in the ambulance?"

"Yes. I imagine she'll be in contact soon," Anthony said. He lifted his chin and placed it against Olivia's stomach as she continued to string her fingers through his hair. "Have you heard from Chelsea?"

"No. I haven't." Olivia buzzed her lips. "Today feels like a nightmare."

"It's good you came. Mary was flustered and as you can see, I'm hiding," Anthony said.

Olivia heaved a sigh. "I'll keep making the rounds outside and make sure everyone is taken care of. We'll keep this place going, no matter what. We've done too much to let it crumble."

"You're a good hotelier."

"I'm just green," Olivia replied with a grin. "I have no idea what I'm doing and making it up as I go along."

The hours stretched on. Olivia ran herself ragged as she spoke with guests about Mr. Adams, about how they didn't know his state yet. She greeted everyone warmly, remembered everyone's names, and shared glasses of wine with several of the guests, all of whom told her that this was something they particularly loved about The Hesson House. "There's a personalized touch here that you don't find elsewhere."

By the time eight o'clock arrived, Olivia shook with a sense of dread. She leaned against the side of the banister on the back porch of The Hesson House and gripped it till her knuckles turned porcelain. Anthony appeared at the bottom of the staircase. His smile reached ear to ear.

"I just got a call from Mrs. Adams," he explained.

"And?" Her heart raced.

"He's all right, and they've stabilized him. They'll be back in a few days to pick up their things, and then they'll head home," Anthony finished, letting out the air he seemed to be holding.

Olivia flung herself down the small staircase and wrapped her arms around Anthony. She held him in a tight embrace for what felt like a small eternity. When she leaned back, the wind off the ocean caught the tears in her eyes.

They made a small announcement to the bar and dining area that Mr. Adams would be all right. Celebratory drinks were ordered, as was another round of tapas. Anthony pointed a firm finger toward Olivia and said, "I know you well enough to know you haven't eaten enough today. You've been too worried about everyone else but yourself."

Olivia felt on the verge of shattering. Anthony laced his fingers through her hand and led her toward a large table near the boat house, which had recently been cleared. Several candles flickered, protected with Bell jars. Olivia sat just as one of the servers arrived to pour her a glass of wine.

"I don't deserve any of this," she said to Anthony in a lilting voice.

"Oh, but yes, you do. And you have guests." Anthony turned and beckoned, and then, as if from a dream, Jennifer, Mila, Camilla, and a pregnant Amelia appeared at the edge of the little beach bar. Olivia had never seen a more beautiful sight.

"Oh!" She leaped up again and hugged each of them.

"We heard you had a hard day today," Amelia said as she collapsed in the chair alongside her. "Anthony called us in for moral support."

"All is clear now. Well, almost." Olivia lifted her phone to check on Chelsea; still no answer. She'd informed the others of the Tyler-Chelsea incident via their group chat and their curiosity burned through the expressions on their faces.

"Still no word from Chels?" Camilla asked as she took a chair across from them.

"I don't know what's wrong," Olivia admitted. "It's driving me nuts. Today has been a huge lesson in not being able to control anything."

"I don't know how to let anything go," Amelia offered with a laugh. "I imagine my head would have blown off by now had I been in your shoes."

"Earlier this afternoon, I heard sirens coming from this direction, and my heart just sank into my stomach," Mila said as she crossed and uncrossed her arms. "I was so worried."

"Well, we made it through another storm," Olivia said, even as tears welled in her eyes. "I feel like I might crack open from stress, but hey. Nothing a glass of wine can't fix. Right?"

Her best friends exchanged worried glances. Olivia snuck a long sip of her wine, then turned her attention toward Camilla, who'd just confessed that Jonathon had forced them into getting a puppy.

"Well, maybe force is the wrong word," Camilla admitted with a laugh. "I told him — we just got Andrea out of the house, and now you want another baby? And he said, yes. So, now, we have this little golden retriever running all over the house and getting hair everywhere. And to be honest with you, I couldn't be happier."

The conversation bubbled after that. They ordered tapas, freshly baked bread, a charcuterie board that had a mixture of cheese, cured meats, olives, nuts and fruits and they ate until their hearts were content, grateful for one another at the end of another wild day. It was mid-September — the end of summer officially and they were headed toward fall, then winter and whatever madness those seasons would throw their way. Either way, Olivia was ready for it.

CHAPTER SIX

"THE THING about Romeo is that he's aggressive. He's dominant. He knows what he wants and how to get it. That's why I'm pretty sure Romeo is an Aries." Olivia glanced up from the paper a student had actually written and turned in for an assignment as Anthony burst into laughter across her at the breakfast table.

"Romeo! An Aries!" Anthony's grin widened. "I've never heard anything so funny in my life."

"I can't believe she thought this was what I meant when I said, 'Write me your thoughts about the dynamic between Romeo and Juliet.'"

"Well, you did keep it pretty open-ended," Anthony pointed it.

"True."

"And does she go on to make good points about why she thinks Romeo is an Aries?"

"She even goes on to say she thinks Juliet is a Pisces and that a

Pisces and an Aries seem good together at first but burn out fast. I guess in a sense, she has her bases covered," Olivia returned.

"What do you think? I think you should give her an A. Maybe an A-plus."

Olivia scrunched her nose, lifted her red pen and poised it over the paper. Anthony drummed his hands on the table in expectation.

"You have all this power over them. You're kind of like their God."

"I know. It's terrifying," Olivia admitted. "And yet—" Here, she drew a B across the top corner of the page and wrote, "Please include more literary themes next time — although I appreciate the creativity."

"Aw. A B?" Anthony clucked his tongue. He then took the pen from Olivia and drew a plus sign next to the B, making it a B plus. "That's better."

"Fine, but she doesn't deserve any favors," Olivia returned.

"Hey, don't mess around with her. She has the secrets of the stars behind her," Anthony returned.

Olivia leaned back and cracked her neck. She had graded fifteen papers that morning and only had seven more to go. After that, she and Anthony had agreed to take a day off from The Hesson House and head to her parents' for a family dinner. The idea of many hours without a single notion of, *"Does suite four have enough towels?"* or *"Why are we already out of vodka for the week?"* felt delicious.

Olivia's phone buzzed with a message from Chelsea. They'd been in contact for the previous two days, ever since Chelsea had finally fessed up that Tyler would stay with her for a little while until he figured out what to do, whatever that meant for a grown man twenty years his daughter's senior. In the text, Chelsea had attached a photograph of her and Tyler at brunch. Both had ordered eggs Benedict; Tyler drank a Bloody Mary. Figures.

"What's up? Your face got all sour all of a sudden."

Olivia flashed the photo around for Anthony to see. He scratched at his chest and said, "I don't know. They look happy at least?"

"Yeah, they do." Maybe this was why it bothered Olivia so much. She was jealous.

Still, she really did feel that Chelsea always gave her father far too many chances. Where was the line? It was always so blurred when it was someone you loved.

AT AROUND FOUR THAT AFTERNOON, Olivia and Anthony discovered her parents, Kim and Dave, out on the back of their wrap-around porch, both a bit loose from their mid-day mimosas. Kim beamed at her daughter and rose up, gesturing out and saying, "Isn't it so beautiful for September? We got lucky."

Olivia rolled herself into her mother's hug and exhaled deeply. After all the hectic energy of the previous weeks, she hadn't realized just how much she'd needed her mother.

"Your brother and Maxine and the kids are almost here," Kim said as she stepped back and straightened herself. After a giggle, she added, "And to be honest with you, I've hardly thought about the food I meant to prepare."

"Let's just order pizza?" Olivia tried.

"Oh, nonsense. I'm the grandmother of this group. I'm meant to cook," Kim demanded, just before she drew up a big burst of energy and stormed into the house.

"I guess I'll head in after her," Olivia said to Anthony and her father, who'd already begun to swap baseball stories from games they'd previously attended over the years. Maybe another woman would have rolled her eyes, but she felt so tender toward the idea that her parents had welcomed Anthony into the fold without pause. They'd never been particularly taken with Tyler and the fact that he had left her hadn't exactly added fire to the idea that Olivia was particularly "good" at all that love stuff. Anthony was different. Anthony planned to stick around.

Well, at least, she hoped.

"So, tell me." Her mother went through the cabinets and pulled out pots and pans and cutting boards. "How is our Chelsea girl?"

Olivia's throat tightened. "You know Chelsea. She's about as headstrong as ever."

"I do know that," Kim replied with a laugh. "Even when she was a little girl, remember? She was so quick-witted and snarky. She never let anyone give her any guff. I'm sure the city won't know what to do with her."

Olivia was silent as she collected a number of onions and began to peel and chop. Her mother flicked on the stereo and played an old *Ace of Base* CD. It was a funny thing, seeing a CD in a CD player — as though they'd stepped back in time.

The door cracked open and Jared hollered out in greeting. Olivia rushed to the doorway and waved an onion-ed hand toward him as he held open the door for Maxine and his kids, Troy and Tessa. The four of them were utterly wholesome. As was her normal duty, Maxine held a tray of baked goods, which she had baked only that afternoon, to ensure they were fresh.

"Hi, there! There's our hotelier," Jared said as he stepped behind his family and headed with them toward the back porch. "Mom put you to work already?"

"You know a lady's duties are never done," Olivia returned.

"I'll be in in a minute," Maxine called.

Kim arched a brow toward Olivia and muttered, "I really like my time alone with my girl, but — I guess we'll let Maxine join in."

Olivia remembered this dynamic between herself and Tyler's mother. She'd just never quite fit with her, like a glove a few sizes too big.

Maxine's energy shifted the mood considerably, it was true, but at least the topic of Chelsea was taken off the table. Maxine had endless things to say about Troy, who was seventeen and now in his senior year.

"I'm surprised you don't have him in class, Liv," Maxine said as she popped open a bottle of wine.

"Maybe he requested to have the other teacher," Olivia said with a sneaky smile. "So I can't keep watch on my nephew."

"Oh! Watch?" Maxine laughed raucously, as though her son had never done a thing wrong in his life.

Olivia, of course, heard rumors. Troy wasn't a bad kid — far from it, but he occasionally ran around with the kids who liked to party, and he'd certainly broken a few girls' hearts. If Maxine had heard tell of this, she wouldn't have believed it. She was too pure of heart.

Maxine headed off briefly to speak with her daughter, which left Olivia and Kim again in the kitchen, a den of their own secrets and gossip. Kim dropped morsels of garlic into the sizzling oil and pushed it around with the spatula.

"You're looking tired, Olivia."

"Gee. Thanks, Mom."

Kim's eyes found Olivia's as she furrowed her brow. "I don't mean it like that. You look beautiful as ever, but I'm worried about you. Jennifer's mother told me that you came into the Frosted Delights crying the other morning."

Olivia rolled her eyes into the back of her head. Had Ariane been in the kitchen without her noticing? Or had Jennifer passed along this information? It didn't matter. All that did was that Martha's Vineyard was too darn small.

"I'm fine, Mom. I just got a bit overwhelmed that day. It was one thing after another. It's just what the hotel industry is and with me juggling both, it can be a lot."

"I understand that. But as far as I've known the past twenty years, you've been a teacher."

"Yes. And now, I'm both."

Kim chuckled. "And when do you take time for yourself, then?" She said it as though she already knew the answer.

Know it all, Olivia thought then.

And, of course, this sizzling inner-voice sarcasm seemed very Chelsea-like behavior. Like grandmother, like mother, like daughter.

"I think it'll calm down after the first year or so," Olivia affirmed. "And I can do anything for a year."

Anthony came in through the kitchen then. His hand draped over Olivia's lower back as he asked her where they had put the bottles of wine they'd bought specifically for the family dinner.

Olivia gazed lovingly up at him as she answered. Anthony then turned to catch sight of Kim, stirring the sauce for the pasta.

"Smells amazing, Kim."

Kim scoffed playfully. "You have to say that."

"I do," Anthony returned. "But it doesn't mean it isn't true."

Kim beamed at him as he stepped back out to find the wine. She then caught Olivia's eye yet again and said, "Well, I suppose if you burn out over the next year, at least you have that man to take you out of the fire."

"Mom..."

"What? I always prayed for you to find a man like him."

"Mom..." Her smile was infectious.

"And you look different," Kim continued.

"I know. You told me already. I look tired."

"No. You look like you're in love. It's a different kind of love than you used to have with that other rascal. That guy. Ugh." She physically shuddered, then continued to stir. "Good thing we got Chelsea out of it. Otherwise, that Tyler character would be totally useless."

Olivia felt as though she slept-walked through much of the rest of dinner. Laughter bubbled through her; her stomach filled and her heart lifted, but by the time nine o'clock hit, her head found Anthony's shoulder and she was knocked out cold. He woke her a few minutes later and gently told her they would drive home now. Olivia hardly recognized where she was.

"Uh oh. We've got patient zero of the zombie apocalypse here," her father said.

"Ugh. Jeez. Did I fall asleep at the table?"

"You did," Jared said. "And we'll never let you forget it."

"Great," Olivia breathed.

She kissed and hugged everyone goodbye, then laced her hands with Anthony's and forced herself out toward the road, where Anthony had parked the car near the mailbox. Again, en route home, she crashed hard, and Anthony threatened to carry her into bed.

"I can make it. I can make it!" she cried as he tried to dig his arms beneath her thighs and lift her through the air.

But a few minutes later, once her head hit the pillow, she was mostly dead to the world. And when her alarm called her out of her sleep at six the following morning, she looked to the next week with dread.

CHAPTER SEVEN

CHELSEA'S FATHER waved a hand out as they parted ways three blocks from Chelsea's apartment. On cue, like some kind of circus performer, Chelsea sent her house keys in a parabola, directly into her father's outstretched palm.

"Thanks, hun," he said, just as automatically as ever, as though they'd done this key exchange more than just the week. "You get off tonight around eleven, you said?"

"Yeah, around then. But only if we don't get a crazy rush."

"Okay, and Xav?"

"He won't be back till late."

Tyler scrunched a hand into a fist and pumped it. "I guess I have your palace all to myself, then."

Chelsea's nostrils flared the slightest bit. Her father didn't even notice it. "Don't have any parties," she told him in a sing-song voice. She wanted him to think she was cool with all of this, that his crashing for the previous week had been a wonderful reprieve, a beautiful reunion. And sure, there had been moments. They'd shared laughter and swapped stories and gone on long walks across the city, exploring. But all the while, Xavier had grown increasingly shadowed. He hardly looked her in the eye when he went to bed at night and got up in the morning. And when she texted him during his work shift, he waited hours to return her messages.

Now, she'd agreed to meet with him as he headed out of work and she headed in. She hadn't told her father about this agreement.

Chelsea walked to Xavier's work with her hands shoved deep in her pockets. She played music through her headphones, sad songs that made her heart shiver with sorrow and just before she arrived at the corner where they'd agreed to share a bagel, Olivia texted her yet again. It had seemed non-stop the previous week. Her mother was hungry to know the ins and outs of Tyler's sudden arrival. It took every bit of strength she had to keep her mother on that island.

MOM: How are you today? You have a shift tonight?

Chelsea began to write back but soon deposited her phone back in her backpack and told herself to get to it later. She had bigger fish to fry. As if on cue, Xavier walked out from the door about a half-block away. When his eyes found hers, he didn't smile. Chelsea forced hers to die immediately. When they met one another, face-to-face, in the center of the sidewalk, Chelsea wanted to make a joke about how they already looked like those constantly upset, near-divorce New Yorkers who walked their dogs around the park without saying a single word.

"Hey," she said instead.

"Hey."

They didn't speak again for another eight minutes until after their bagel, cheese, and egg sandwich had been crafted and Xavier had paid the full seven-fifty it cost. They sat on a bench overlooking a little park, where a child stormed toward his mother, who texted, bored.

"Nature versus technology, I guess," Chelsea joked.

Xavier didn't laugh. This was normally the kind of joke he would have loved. Chelsea's tongue felt sour, and she refused the first bite of the bagel. Xavier just held it upright as though they both waited for the other to speak first.

Finally, Xavier leaped.

"He's been here the entire week, Chels."

"I know." She heaved a sigh. "I know."

"And you didn't even ask me before you told him he could sleep on the couch. You just let it happen."

"I know."

"What am I supposed to do with that?"

"I don't know."

Again, silence. Xavier dropped his hands so that the bagel now sat gently on the bench between them. Only a few weeks before, they would have thrown themselves at one another on the bench, making out for all the world to see. Now, it was like they were strangers.

"Do you have any idea how much longer he wants to stay with us?"

"I haven't asked."

"Do you know if he's talked to Casey at all?"

"I don't think he has."

"Jesus, Chels."

Chelsea's eyes filled with tears. She had resolved, a long time ago, never to lie to Xavier. There on that bench, she gave him only honesty and she hated it. All she wanted to do was tell him, "Just a few more days," or, "I'll go home right now and tell him he has to get out." But she knew in her heart that she couldn't. Where her father was concerned, she was handicapped. She loved him so completely; she needed him to love her with every ounce of who she was. It wasn't bigger than her and Xavier's relationship, exactly; it had just gone on a whole lot longer.

Xavier stood and began to pace in front of the bench. The child far beyond in the park had ultimately stolen his mother's cell phone and banged it against the grass. The mother's shoulders slumped forward in defeat, much like Chelsea's did, now.

"This was supposed to be our big chance to start fresh," Xavier said then. "Here in New York, just you and me. And now, this? And you're just going along with it like it's no big deal?"

"It is a big deal. I know it is." Chelsea closed her eyes. Anger and fear and sorrow swirled in her stomach. "Why would you think I don't think it's a big deal?"

"You just let him walk all over you."

"You mean, the way I'm letting you walk all over me right now?" Chelsea stood up and glared at him.

Xavier stopped pacing. They locked eyes. Neither spoke for a full thirty seconds.

"My father is in trouble," Chelsea blurted. "I know you kind of hate your parents, or whatever, but I don't hate mine. We're all just people trying to figure things out, and we're always supposed to have our family's backs. Why shouldn't I be there for him?"

"I just don't think you understand how much he's manipulating you," Xavier blurted.

"Are you kidding me?" Chelsea's eyes bulged out. "That's so, so awful to hear. Do you know how awful you're being?"

"I'm just telling the truth."

"Yeah? Take your truth somewhere else," Chelsea returned. She took a huge step away from him just as he reached out in an attempt to grab her hand. "Don't touch me. I don't want to talk to you."

"We came here today to talk about this. If we just abandon it, then what does that say about our relationship?"

"I don't know, Xavier. What do you think it says?" Chelsea's words were volatile. She grabbed her bag and shot away from him, headed for the main road. She shook violently as she walked. When she rounded the corner, she paused for a moment, listening for Xavier's footfalls, but none came. He had decided not to come after her, of course.

He didn't care. Not as much as she did. This was proof, and she didn't need anything else.

Chelsea was at a total loss. She wandered the streets and pointed herself in the direction of Tiny Tim's. But ultimately, when she reached the subway stop, she texted her boss, Marty, to tell him she was puking and wouldn't make it.

CHELSEA: My doc says it's walking pneumonia. I can't come to work for about a week.

CHELSEA: I'm as upset as you are. I need that money.

CHELSEA: Please, don't fire me.

It took Marty a full four minutes to text back, even though she knew he was perpetually glued to his phone at this hour of the day.

MARTY: You're kidding me, right?

CHELSEA: 'fraid not, coach.

MARTY: Okay. If it's longer than a week, I have to take you off the schedule for good.

CHELSEA: Thank you.

Chelsea hustled down the steps of the subway station. She no longer had any control over her limbs. In a flash, she made her way into the relevant train, then gripped the side of the bustling car as it chugged her toward the bus station. She arrived at the bus just as the driver drew his doors closed. She banged on the glass, and he finally let her in, making sure to grumble about it the entire time.

She was off to Boston, where she would make a change-over, which would ultimately take her to Woods Hole, Massachusetts.

From there, she would take the ferry home.

Her mind went about a million places during that first bus ride to Boston. She sat with her forehead leaned up against the glass and thought about Xavier, about how much she had thought he was the one, the one to change her life for good. She thought about how he had looked at her back at that park, as though she was some kind of symbol of evil itself. She thought, too, of what he'd said about her father, about his manipulation. She knew he was right.

But she couldn't face him or tell him that.

And she couldn't fess up to it to Xavier, either.

Perhaps a few months ago, she could have. But just then, she felt exhausted, as though the world had decided to move onto her shoulders and press her down with all its might.

An autumn rain fluttered its droplets across the glass of the bus. She placed her hand over the glass and watched as the speed of the rain escalated. The clouds overhead were thick and rolling over the top of one another, in some kind of race. A man off to the left of her in the bus grunted about an approaching storm. Somehow, Chelsea had forgotten about these typical autumn storms — the ones that told you, beyond any shadow of a doubt, that summer and all its beauty had ceased. It was time to be inside and let nature take its course.

Chelsea checked her phone. It was just past four-thirty, but she still had a long journey ahead. Marty texted her again to say it was too bad she couldn't come into work since one of her regulars had come. He always tipped her upwards of forty percent. Chelsea cursed herself inwardly; she needed that cash.

But, right then, she needed one person on the planet. She needed her mother. For too long, she had shoved Olivia as far away as she could and now it was time to change that.

She texted her mother just to get a sense of her schedule. It was better to surprise her, after all. She wanted to make those tears fall.

CHELSEA: Hey Mom! How's your day going? I heard the east might get some kind of storm.

Olivia wrote back almost immediately.

OLIVIA: Hey, hun. Yeah. I got out of work a little while ago and I'm about to head over to the hotel. I'm watching the clouds now. Kind of ominous. How's the city?

Chelsea knew her mother wanted nothing more than to ask, "How's Tyler?" She'd held it in for Chelsea's sake.

CHELSEA: Not bad. Are you going to be at the hotel all night?

OLIVIA: All night, every night. Your grandmother said I look "tired," lol.

CHELSEA: Grandma has a way with words, doesn't she?

OLIVIA: Something like that.

OLIVIA: Gotta run. I hope this storm doesn't hit us too hard. Scary!

OLIVIA: Love you.

CHELSEA: Love you, too, Mom.

Chelsea pressed her phone against her chest. At that moment, Xavier texted her.

XAVIER: Hey. I came to your work to talk to you and they said you're at home sick.

XAVIER: What the heck.

XAVIER: I called your dad. He says you're not there, either.

XAVIER: Chelsea. Where are you?

XAVIER: Chelsea. Please.

Chelsea turned her phone on Airplane mode after that. She then stuck her air buds into her ears, leaned her head back, and continued to watch the rain. Just recently, she'd "run away from home," from the island to NYC. Now, she ran right back.

But there was freedom in making this decision. Nobody could tell her it was the right thing or the wrong thing to do. It just was.

And soon, she would look her mother in the eye and tell her — well. She wasn't fully sure she could muster, "You were right." But maybe she could come up with something similar. Maybe.

CHAPTER EIGHT

OLIVIA'S PHONE buzzed with non-stop messages from Mila, Camilla, Jennifer, and Amelia. A storm was approaching and there was no telling what would happen next. The weather forecast said it had the potential of turning into a tropical storm and then transitioning into hurricane status. She'd heard the announcement last week, but it had slipped her mind with all the other issues going on. Now, the island was suddenly in a frenzy. Olivia's mission was to drive as quickly as she could to The Hesson House and ensure that her guests were all right. Anthony and Mary were already there, battening down the hatches in preparation for the coming torrential rains and wind. Anthony only had time to send her one message: Get here sooner than later.

Olivia sat in the front seat of her car as the rain peppered over the glass. She had just enough time to read through her texts as her engine buzzed and the radio spat out frantic words from the radio announcer, telling everyone on Martha's Vineyard and surrounding areas to take shelter.

AMELIA: I'm so glad I stocked up over the summer. I have provisions for days.

CAMILLA: You're always so prepared. Jonathon says if we run out of food, we're doomed.

AMELIA: I'll swim over and bring you a can of tuna if it comes to that.

MILA: You guys! I'm terrified. The wind is insane. I hate that my babies are off to college…

OLIVIA: Is Liam with you?

MILA: He's on his way. I hope he gets here fast.

OLIVIA: I'm glad you won't be alone.

JENNIFER: And you, Liv? Where are you going to be?

OLIVIA: The Hesson House. I have to be.

JENNIFER: Just remember to keep yourself safe. Don't do anything rash.

CAMILLA: I love all of you so much! Be safe! It's starting to get wild out there!

The windshield wipers struggled through the frantic rain as she drove slowly toward The Hesson House. She parked and hustled up the front steps, where she burst into the foyer. Her hair streaked her forehead and her cheeks, and when she flashed past the mirror, she caught a brief image of a forty-year-old woman turned wet-rat.

"Anthony!" She spotted him in the dining room, where he had positioned the slats over the windows for protection. Several of the guests remained in the dining room, sipping wine and watching as the clouds rolled toward them. They were all bowling pins at the far end of a bowling alley, and the clouds were prepared for a strike.

Anthony's eyes were large, as though they'd tried to swallow the entire sky whole.

"How's it going?" Olivia asked under her breath. She didn't want to frighten the guests, even as their conversation bubbled and spat with their opinions on what to do regarding the storm.

"We've got almost everything covered," Anthony told her. "Gosh, you're pale."

Olivia swallowed the lump in her throat. "During difficult storms in the past, I've just had Chelsea to look after. Now, I feel responsible for all these people here at the edge of the island. It's terrifying, to say the least."

"We're far enough away from the water that I think we'll be fine," Anthony said. "And we made sure the library in the back is secure enough to hold all our guests, for situations just like this. We even talked about it all the way back in March. You remember?"

Olivia remembered when they had sat down together to craft a hurricane-tropical-storm plan. At the time, the concept had seemed so far away. The spring sunshine had glittered in through the kitchen windows, and they had shared kisses through coffee sips. Now, the nightmare had stormed toward them.

An older woman stood on rickety legs and tapped Olivia on the shoulder.

"I don't mean to bother you, Mrs. Hesson," she said softly. "But what are we meant to do if this storm turns into something a little more — shall we say, deadly?"

Olivia formed a generous smile, even as her heart shattered

with fear. "We have a plan in place, of course. But just now, the storm is far enough away that we should be fine. Why don't you sit down? It's the perfect time for a cocktail, isn't it?" Olivia guided the woman back to her seat, alongside her sister, who was also in her seventies. They both ordered vodka tonics, and Olivia reported she'd be back in a jiffy. By the time she fled back toward the bartender, the sisters had begun to shuffle the deck of cards between them. Maybe this early evening could turn into one like all the others, with just the added drama of "what if a storm turns into a hurricane and swallows them all whole?"

Olivia walked to every table in the dining area and greeted everyone warmly, telling them that for now, everything was all clear, but they would report when and if it was time to gather in their "safe room," where they would be protected from harsh winds. Olivia knew better than to use the F-word (flood) as she knew that would generate a kind of frenzy. Between stop-overs at tables, she found it very difficult to breathe. Eventually, she and Anthony met with some of the other staff members in the kitchen, where she poured them all whiskey shots and said, "Let's keep ourselves and the guests safe. Here goes nothing." They tossed the shots back, then joined hands and prayed as the winds grew louder, more demanding.

"Bless this hotel. Bless the guests within it," Olivia breathed.

Hours passed. There was a frenetic energy over the table-tops, and conversation bubbled and spat — as though everyone anticipated coming disaster and wanted to get the last word in.

Anthony and Olivia stepped outside to readjust one of the window shields. Out there, the wind thrust itself against their backs and tore at their hair.

"This wind is really crazy. I wonder how much stronger it's going to get," Olivia hollered, barely loud enough to be heard over the storm.

Anthony clicked the shield over the top part of the window, turned around, and "whooped" toward the water. The sound of his cries joined with the wind and the rain; he sounded like a wild man. Olivia joined him. It was the first time she'd been able to scream like this — really scream in a way that represented all the stress and anxiety and fear of the previous few months. It was freeing. It was the pinnacle of therapy. And because of the storm, nobody could hear her.

Anthony turned and scooped his arms around her and kissed her as the rain turned sideways and barreled against them. Olivia's eyes closed with the kiss. And for a moment, as the world spun around them and threatened to collapse, she felt completely free.

But there wasn't time for this. Their kiss broke, and Anthony hustled Olivia back inside, where they inspected themselves in the mirror, the wet curls and Olivia's black makeup-stained cheeks. She mopped herself up and checked her phone again.

A news report stated that already, the storm had been deemed a tropical storm.

"We need to get everyone to the library," she told Anthony. "Let's make sure everyone's out of their rooms."

Anthony nodded and headed off through the kitchen. Olivia informed the staff within the kitchen, along with any approaching maid she spotted in the hall. Once in the dining and bar area, she found terribly quiet guests with their eyes to their phones as they read about the swift shift of the storm.

"Everyone! Can I have your attention, please?" This was

Olivia's teacher's voice, one of confidence. Finally, it came in handy outside of the classroom. "We're going to need everyone to gather in the library, which is our safe room for occasions just like this. The Hesson House is far up from the water, enough so that we should be all right. This is just a precaution. And know that we've put every storm protection in place. You and your families and friends will be just fine."

Olivia wondered what, exactly, someone like her had said on the Titanic. Had it been something like this? *"You'll all be fine! We've taken every precaution! This boat can't sink!"* Ugh. She suddenly felt connected to every natural disaster across the world, across history.

The guests stepped toward the library. Olivia eased back to ensure some of the older guests made their way without stumbling. Anthony bopped around upstairs, heading from room to room and calling for everyone else to return downstairs. They had thirty-seven guests amongst them that day and Olivia planned to bring all thirty-seven guests through to the end of the line, no matter what.

Once at the library, Olivia told everyone to make themselves comfortable. This wasn't easy, as there were only three couches and a handful of chairs. Several people sat on the floor and crossed their legs uncomfortably. Olivia hustled back to the front desk, where she scrounged around for toys and board games and decks of cards. She brought her supplies back and smiled as brightly as she could. She wanted to say something like, "No reason we can't make this fun, right?" But she held it in—no use feigning excitement during a terrifying time.

Six other guests padded down the circular staircase, followed by Anthony, who'd herded them like a sheep dog. His eyes locked with Olivia as he said, "That's the last of them."

"Wonderful," she said as she smiled at the other guests, three of whom seemed to have only just been yanked from their sleep. "Right this way, everyone." She guided them into the library, where they found seats in the corner. She was grateful to find several of the guests had built up a card game together, introducing themselves and chatting gently, despite the fear in their eyes.

Olivia hurried back into the foyer, latching the door behind her. "Is there anything else we should do?" Olivia demanded of Anthony.

"I don't think so. I mean, I can't think of anything," Anthony said.

"I know. I just keep thinking of afterward. Like, will there be something we say, 'Oh, I can't believe we forgot that! It would have changed everything!'"

"I think we've done everything we can. Except take cover ourselves."

Olivia headed to the door nearest the foyer and peered out. The wind barreled at the trees and forced them toward the ground. All she could think of at this moment was the first time she'd ever seen this big house. She and Tyler had come as teenagers to make out there for the first time. It had seemed endlessly majestic and filled with secrets. In the previous months, she'd been so diligent — careful to keep the old-world detail as she and Anthony built it back up to its former glory.

Suddenly, a big truck pulled up outside of the mansion. Olivia's heart swelled with terror.

"Who is out driving right now? Did you send someone out for something?" she demanded of Anthony.

Anthony shook his head. Olivia whipped open the door and then watched as a teenage girl burst out of the passenger side. Her hair whipped out behind her and was immediately drenched. And when her eyes lifted, Olivia's heart dropped into the bottom of her gut.

There, rushing up the steps of the hotel, was her daughter.

It was Chelsea.

Olivia hustled out from the door, even as Anthony called for her to come back. In a flash, she wrapped her arms around her daughter as the tropical storm winds wrapped around them and threatened to take them down. Olivia hadn't a single clue why her daughter was there that evening. Perhaps the storm winds were so strong that they'd opened up some kind of portal and allowed Olivia to protect the most important person in her world.

"Come on!" Anthony called. His hand wrapped around Olivia's elbow and tugged at her. Olivia drew her daughter into the foyer, then turned back and watched as the man who'd driven the truck, a man who looked to be from the docks, hustled in after them.

"Chelsea. What the heck?" Olivia cried just as the dock worker burst through the foyer, a wide grin across his cheeks.

The dock worker locked eyes with Chelsea as he blared, "That has got to be the best one hundred dollars I've ever made. She dangled those bills in front of me and said, 'I'll pay big if you get me all the way to The Hesson House before the storm really kicks off. And I said, hell yeah."

CHAPTER NINE

BUT IN THE FOYER, Olivia wrapped her arms around her daughter yet again and demanded, "What the heck got into you? Why the heck are you here? Chelsea?" Her heart thumped against her ribcage and threatened to crack itself through. Chelsea shivered against her as Anthony's words boomed, "We need to get in the library. Right now!" His hand-stretched across Olivia's and pressed her toward the room, where she watched as the dock worker already took up residence at one of the tables and demanded to be a part of the board game. Everyone looked at this man dripping wet from the storm, burly from long hours at the dock and decided not to make a fuss about starting over. Anthony latched the door closed behind them and gaped at Chelsea. She was the prodigal daughter.

"Come on," Olivia whispered. She slipped her fingers through her daughter's and rushed her toward the far corner of the library, where they were hidden by a large shelf of books. Once there, she hugged her daughter all over again, then lifted the bottle of whiskey from her purse. "I can't believe all this time that I've thought I only had to worry about my friends and family and the hotel guests. But you were out there? Traveling from New York City? And paying some dock worker to bring you all the way here from Oak Bluffs?"

Chelsea's eyes sparkled mischievously. "It worked, didn't it?"

"It sure as heck shouldn't have." Olivia poured them small shots, which they clinked quietly. Her eyes felt glazed over with fear. "Chelsea. Why are you here?"

Outside, the wind pressed itself like a thick blanket against the side of the mansion. Chelsea's eyes searched the space around them.

"I should have checked the weather before my spontaneous trip home, I guess."

"That's just your generation, isn't it? Endlessly optimistic about your plans," Olivia teased.

Chelsea shrugged. "I wouldn't want you to go through this alone."

Olivia furrowed her brow. Her daughter hadn't said such kind words to her in quite a while — words that suggested that the two of them were more like a team.

"Your dad. I didn't want to pry..." Olivia began.

Chelsea's eyes hardened slightly. "Can we talk about this after the hurricane sweeps us away?"

Anthony ambled around the bookshelf and crossed his arms nervously. "The guests are growing nervous and more annoying by the second if you can believe it."

"We have that stock of wine here in the library," Olivia pointed out. "And there are those boxes of coffee mugs in the cabinet. Let's make it a little party."

Anthony nodded and turned back toward the kitchen staff, who assisted him with finding the crates of wine and the mugs. Olivia and Chelsea stepped out from the back of the library and huddled together, listening as the wind smashed around them. There was so much to say, so much they'd buried beneath the surface.

"Crap. The phones just went out," Olivia said as she checked her cell. "I wanted to text the girls to see if everyone was okay."

"Ugh. Well, to be honest, not having a phone right now is beneficial for me," Chelsea admitted.

"Didn't you have work tonight?" Olivia asked.

Chelsea shrugged flippantly. Olivia knew better than to press the matter.

As this seemed a bit like "the end of the world," it was fascinating to eavesdrop on others' conversations in the library. The seventy-something-year-old sisters got into a funny argument, bickering about something that had happened all the way back in the seventies.

"You told Jeffrey that you wish you'd married him instead of Ollie," one of them said pointedly. "I'm tired of you pretending that you didn't say that. He was my husband! What made you think that was okay?"

"Oh, God, Mary-Anne. Are we really going to get back on that?" the other demanded.

"When you insinuated to the father of my children that you wished you would have built a life with him instead of your own husband? Yes, we're going to get back on that," the other retorted.

Mary-Anne countered wickedly. "Then why the heck did we spend all that money on therapy in the nineties if we're just going to keep bringing it up again and again? You said you were over it!

Besides, Jeffrey died ten years ago, and Ollie died two years ago. It's just you and me, babe. You and me till the end and maybe this is it!" She raised her mug of wine and waggled her eyebrows.

Chelsea squeezed her mother's wrist hard and seemed to suppress endless giggles.

Alongside the bickering sisters, the dock worker continued to play a terribly competitive game of Life alongside a family of four and another straggler.

"I don't see the benefit of going to college," the dock worker informed one of the younger girls from the family as she toyed with the card in her hand. "I mean, you could make money immediately and then buy whatever you want."

The young girl's mother and father glowered at the dock worker. "I don't think that tells the whole story," the mother said, careful not to say anything too dark, as she didn't want to insult the fact that the dock worker had never gone to school.

"It's marriage and babies for me this time around," the dock worker said. He then turned his head toward Chelsea and actually winked at her.

"Chelsea. You made the dock worker fall in love with you. During a tropical storm," Olivia said.

"Actually, right before I came in, it switched to a hurricane."

"Good to know. Does it have a name yet?"

"Yep. It's called Janine."

"Tropical Storm Janine. Huh." Olivia had just met a woman named Janine — Janine Grimson, who had just arrived on the island in June after her life had crumbled in Manhattan.

"It's not a bad name. Sometimes, they come up with the weirdest names," Chelsea said thoughtfully.

"You're changing the subject. What's the deal with the dock worker?" Olivia asked under her breath as she watched as the dock worker slipped a little pink figurine into his Life vehicle and clapped his hands.

"Finally! A wife!" he cried.

"I don't know. His name is Tony and he was just there with his truck watching the waves when I got off the boat. I almost didn't make that ferry. Thank goodness we made it all the way from Woods Hole before the storm really picked up."

"And you paid this Tony character one hundred dollars? In cash?"

"Tips add up differently in NYC, Mommy," Chelsea told her. "But everything else hits differently, too."

The storm grew more violent. The lights went out, and several guests shrieked and refilled their mugs of wine. Olivia wrapped her arms around Chelsea and shook violently. Anthony returned with mugs of wine for the three of them, then sat alongside Olivia and held her tightly, too. Olivia was overwhelmed with the love she felt and also with just how terrifying it was to not know what would happen next. Here, she had the two people she loved in the world the most. But she was helpless against nature. She wasn't helpless against time.

She'd long ago understood that everything you loved in the world eventually went away or changed. This had never been an easy thing for her to accept. Her thoughts burned with sorrow. Not today, she thought. Spare us today.

"I don't think we should use the lights going out as a reason to end the game of Life," Tony said to the other players at the table.

They looked at him as though he had three heads.

"Mom?" Chelsea breathed.

"What is it, honey?"

"I'm scared."

"I know. Me too."

There were wicked sounds after that: the creaking of wood both new and old — the trees outside and bits and pieces of the hotel cracking, the beautiful mansion that had withstood so many years of winds. There was the sound of shattering glass, despite all their best efforts. Olivia gripped Chelsea and Anthony's hand so hard that her knuckles turned to a crisp white.

They remained in that room for four hours. At times, Olivia felt it was a version of hell that they'd all been sent there to wait out the rest of eternity. Her heart went out to her parents, to her brother and his family, to her sister off the island, and of course, to her best friends. She prayed they would all be safe and together soon.

When the winds calmed, Anthony announced he would leave the shelter and check. Olivia nearly refused to let his hand go. She gazed lovingly into his eyes and said, "Maybe just a little while longer?"

But Anthony beckoned to the frantic guests and said, "We owe it to them to report what's going on."

Olivia knew he was right. After he released her hand, she threw this open one over Chelsea's, as though she could trick it into believing Anthony remained. Anthony eased out of the shelter door and back into the foyer. Throughout the next ten minutes, during which Anthony wandered around outside of the shelter, Olivia couldn't muster a single word.

Finally, Anthony reappeared in the crack of the door. He beckoned for Olivia and Chelsea and Mary to come with him.

Olivia squeezed Chelsea's hand as the two of them stood and walked softly, gently, toward the door. Once there, Olivia turned back to announce her plans to the guests.

"Hello, everyone. I know it's been a remarkably stressful time for all of us. Thank you for your patience and your cooperation and your bravery. Right now, I'm going to assess the outside and report back to you when we know more. Let's be grateful this wasn't one of the longer ones. I have no way to check the weather, but I remember other storms like this that stretched on from twelve to twenty-four hours. This one just nicked us. And it seems we're all okay. So, everyone just hang in there."

She swallowed the lump in her throat, surprised that she sounded at all comprehensible. Her mind was a tangled mess.

"Keep drinking as much wine as you like. We will provide you with dinner soon," she said.

Dock-worker Tony rubbed his palms together excitedly. He'd won the game of Life, and he'd kept his little car stocked with his two adults and four children, a reminder of the life he'd built in 2-D. Somehow, this made Olivia terribly sad.

Olivia, Mary, and Chelsea followed Anthony into the foyer and clipped the library door closed behind them.

Almost immediately, Olivia felt a scream coil up from her stomach. It threatened to burst from her lips, but she kept it in.

Already, it was clear. The storm had come and threatened to sweep them all away. And it had taken a great deal of The Hesson House along with it.

CHAPTER TEN

THE FIRST DAY after Tyler had left Olivia, Olivia had walked silently through the house they'd once shared as though it were a tomb, and she was sent there to mourn the dead. There, the couch that they once cuddled on through the night as they had flicked through television shows and squabbled over which move to watch; there, where they had watched Chelsea take her first steps and stagger across the carpet; there, where they'd kissed one another over and over, good morning and good night as the days had passed them by. Later, the tomb had eventually returned to its normal state — just another house, a space she and Chelsea had shared. It had lost its sorrows; its memories had faded.

The Hesson House now echoed with ghosts, just as Olivia and Tyler's house had. Olivia gripped Chelsea's hand hard as she blinked out through the now completely open foyer, where the wind had barreled through the front door and broken through even the shields. Water rushed up from the waterline and made the parking lot a sort of stream. This meant that the water had completely obliterated the front beach restaurant area and probably the boathouse along with it. Olivia and Chelsea aligned their stride and marched into the open area of the porch that swung out toward the parking lot, careful to watch for glass beneath them.

The glorious, ancient trees that lined the property had taken a real hit. Many of them remained, with their limbs strewn out along the ground as the water swerved around them. Some others had been ripped up from the ground and cast to the side, like trash.

"Oh no. No, no, no." Olivia muttered to herself, knowing just how un-rational she sounded yet unclear on how to make herself calm.

"It's okay, Mom. We're all okay." Chelsea's words were somber yet clear.

The waters trickled around the vehicles, cutting up about halfway up the tires. Tony's big pickup truck seemed generally unaffected. He would maybe be a blessing yet again, as perhaps he could help drive some of the guests to the ferry — if the ferry was cleared to take people off the island.

"There's much more to see," Anthony said as his eyes found Olivia's. He beckoned for her to follow him through the foyer and then back to the dining room. Much of the dining room was still intact; apparently, their storm shields had worked properly. But when they stepped out onto the back porch, they found one-half of it ripped off and cast to the waters below, which rushed wildly around the property. The hotel now felt like a floating dock.

"This stupid porch," Chelsea said as she bucked back, frightened. She'd broken her leg out there months before and apparently didn't trust it with her weight. Olivia didn't blame her.

"I went upstairs as far as I could, but a lot of that is destroyed," Anthony said with a sigh. "Much of the top floor is obliterated. I think we should be able to get up into the guests' rooms and retrieve their things. There shouldn't be water damage unless the rain got into their rooms."

"Okay. Thank you." Olivia felt faced with a horrific realization that they would soon have to close The Hesson House, perhaps for the foreseeable future. One moment, she had been the proud new owner of The Hesson House, one of the most exclusive and beautiful boutique hotels on the east coast (according to several magazines, all of which had interviewed her since the opening in July).

But now? Now, she was just the owner of a dilapidated hurricane-destroyed sack of bricks and wood and marble. And she had thirty-seven disgruntled guests — all of whom had arrived at Martha's Vineyard for what had been described to them as a "beautiful time of relaxation and refined living." There was nothing refined about being trapped in a library for four hours, playing cards and listening to the wind roar outside.

It didn't matter how much money you had. Nature cared very little about that. It cared very little about your best-laid plans.

Olivia's lower lip quivered as she pondered what to do next. "Does your phone work yet?" she asked Anthony, who shook his head no.

She suddenly felt as though they had crashed their ship into a deserted island. It was still largely impossible to drive to town. Many of their things had been destroyed, and there was no contact with the outside world.

Olivia rushed back to the kitchen, where she found that their pantry and stockpile of food hadn't been touched. They still didn't have electricity, but she would ask the chefs to improvise the best they could.

"Let's set up the dining room as beautifully as we can," she said to Anthony and Chelsea. "It could be the final dinner at The Hesson House — maybe ever."

"Mom..." Chelsea said as she crossed her arms over her chest.

"We don't know. The damage is extraordinary," Olivia said somberly. "I think it's best to go out with a bang."

Olivia returned to the library, where she found all of the guests, the staff members, and Tony, the dock worker standing up, eagerly waiting. When they spotted her, they all breathed a collective sigh of relief.

"Hello, everyone." Olivia's voice wavered just slightly. "It's an unfortunate thing to report, but we don't yet have contact with the outside world, and we need to remain here at the hotel a little while longer. The damage is — well, extensive from what we can see so far. There are no two ways around it. It's enormous. We want to keep you downstairs in the dining room and feed you and let you drink up as long as you like. We'll also bring pillows and blankets in for those of you who wish to sleep."

"What about our things?" one woman cried as she lifted her hand frantically.

"Due to the storm, we're a bit hesitant about the integrity of the house at this time," Olivia explained. "So we don't feel comfortable allowing you to go into your rooms. We can, of course, go up and retrieve anything you might need. Anything of real importance."

The guests exchanged worried glances. Olivia had the overwhelming sensation that they blamed her for the storm — that it had been up to her to keep it at bay, and she'd failed them. She opened the door wider and stepped to the side to allow the guests their mass exodus. As they went, their eyes turned leftward to investigate the enormous hole cut through the foyer. Their gasps were the perfect soundtrack. It really was dire, what they saw.

"Let's all head to the dining area!" Olivia called as they wandered out. "Please, everyone, stick together. Don't leave the premises. Please."

One man paused and disobeyed her, right before her eyes. He cut through the foyer and peered out, then coughed. "My Porsche," he breathed. "The water. It's probably flooded inside."

"You can't think about that right now," Olivia pleaded with him. "The water will go down soon. We're on a hill. It will retreat back to the ocean where it belongs."

"That Porsche is my life," the man told her as his broad shoulders rounded downward.

Olivia yearned to say something pointed here — something like, "I hope your wife knows your car is your entire life." But she kept that at bay, thank goodness.

"Please, sir, can I ask you to head to the dining area with everyone else? We'll know more very soon."

The man looked at her with the cruelest expression she'd ever experienced, then sauntered in after the other guests, grumbling to himself. Probably, he had a choice word or two for Olivia. Probably, she'd read about it in a Google review later. Great.

By some sort of grace of God, the piano, located just on the other side of the foyer, between the library and the dining area, seemed untouched. Olivia placed her fingers delicately on the keys and then created a chord, then another. Her heart surged. When she lifted her eyes toward Chelsea, Chelsea beamed and hustled toward the keys.

"I'll play something," she said.

"Really? I didn't think you'd played in years."

"I've been practicing in New York," Chelsea told her. "There's a piano in the restaurant, and I play after I've finished my duties for the night or before the guests arrive for the first dinner wave."

Chelsea sat at the piano as though she'd performed that very action every day of her life. She wagged her eyebrows, showing off and then churned into an old Billy Joel tune, aptly named "Piano Man."

"Thank you," Olivia breathed, although Chelsea couldn't hear her any longer.

The ambiance shifted considerably. The guests sat at the round tables in the dining room, frequently pairing up with other guests, many of whom they hadn't known previously. There was an air of having survived something, a great catastrophe, and exhausted laughter filled the air. A young woman toward the far end of the dining room began to sing the lyrics of "Piano Man," and several others joined in for a sing-along.

"Sing us a song, you're the piano man!" they cried. "Sing us a song tonight. For we're all in the mood for a melody, and you've got us feeling all right."

The staff of The Hesson House began to rush from the kitchen with bottles of wine and glistening wine glasses, which had miraculously survived the storm. Candles had been lit; still more were brought in from storage. Despite the darkness of this post-storm, everything was suddenly illuminated. Anthony's strong arms wrapped around Olivia's waist, and he held her like that, as though she might fly away along with the tree limbs, and swayed with her in time to the music. Slowly, as the minutes ticked on and Chelsea selected another song, the realization took hold: this was probably it. It was time to make the most out of these memories. The curtain was about to be drawn closed for an unforeseeable amount of time.

Olivia and Anthony spoke with the chef about his plans for the make-shift dinner. "We have a big selection of cured meats, smoked salmon and plenty of fresh vegetables and fruits. We'd only just baked all these baguettes, so we'll send out bowls of sliced bread shortly, along with dips from the fridge. I'll try to use up as much as we can — since I'm guessing..."

Olivia nodded. "You're guessing right. Who knows when we'll serve a meal here again?"

"I just hope we can get these people home safe by tomorrow," her chef said. He smeared a hand across his sweaty forehead and ogled the window, where a full view of the ocean, shimmering up along the porch line, was reflected back. "And I hope phone service comes back soon, too. I need to call some family. I'm guessing you do, too."

Olivia nodded as tears sprung to her eyes. There was no telling what the rest of the island had taken in the rush of this hurricane. Clearly, the storm had rolled on across the ocean — maybe headed for the Carolinas or down for Florida. It was done with them. It had eaten what it wanted and passed on the rest.

"But for right now, we have guests to feed. People to care for," the chef said, echoing Olivia's sentiments exactly. "Which is maybe the best feeling in the world. At a time like this, it's much better to be able to give back. In any way, we can."

"I feel exactly the same," Olivia affirmed.

Dinner was a success. Everywhere Olivia looked, guests ate heartily — smearing homemade dips on freshly-baked bread, sipping wine, feasting on smoked salmon and fresh vegetable sandwiches, and speaking together. It felt like a great celebration. And when she knew all had been fed, Anthony convinced her to sit at one of the round tables with a few other guests and eat her fill, too. Her knees clacked together as she took her first bite. The bread and cheese together were remarkable. Olivia's eyes closed with a mix of sorrow and joy and relief. It had been ages since a single morsel of food had passed her lips.

"What time is it, anyway?" she asked Anthony.

"It's just past one."

"And nobody even looks tired," Olivia said with a laugh.

Tony the dock-worker, who sat on the other side of Chelsea, eating much more than his fill, said that this lack-of-fatigue illustrated a funny thing about people. "People can withstand so much more than they realize," he said between bites. "It's incredible."

Olivia, who couldn't be annoyed or hate anyone at that moment, nodded her head in agreement. He was right.

CHAPTER ELEVEN

PHONE SERVICE RETURNED AROUND six in the morning. Olivia's phone buzzed wildly against her stomach as she slept in the office, spooned beneath Anthony's strong arms, while Chelsea was curled up on the couch near the wall. Olivia lifted her phone to find fifty-seven messages from her friends and family. The messages she'd sent had just arrived on their phones as well. Through the air over the war-torn island, messages sent themselves back and forth — a reminder that once upon a time, things had been normal.

Olivia could make time for the messages later. In the meantime, she had to figure out a way to get these people out of the dining room and off the island. Lucky for her, she had a perfect figure in her corner for the task: Amelia Taylor herself.

Olivia padded out toward the destructed foyer, shivering beneath a big coat she'd nabbed from her office closet. Amelia's phone rang only twice before she answered. Her voice was high-pitched and frantic.

"Thank God it's you!" Amelia cried.

"Amelia! Are you okay?"

"Yes. We're all fine here on Peases Point," Amelia assured her. "Oliver was already over, and we put up all the storm shields and everything. We're a bit too high for the water to get here, but I can only imagine what it's like at The Hesson House."

Olivia was silent for a moment. Amelia heaved a sigh.

"I thought so. I thought the worst," Amelia breathed.

"Everyone is okay. I just need a way to get them out of here."

Sunlight had begun to creep its way from the eastern horizon, casting the grounds in a grey, shimmery light. The water had receded quite a bit; it trickled gently around the vehicles and cast itself back down the hill toward the vast ocean beyond.

"I was hoping you could hire a few buses for me," Olivia suggested. "Send them my way, maybe around nine?"

"On it," Amelia affirmed. "How's the damage?"

"Don't ask."

"Gosh. Okay. Okay." Amelia muttered to herself and then said something a bit louder, off to the side, probably to Oliver. "Have you talked to the other girls?"

"Not yet. Is everyone okay?"

"Yes. Jennifer and Derek, Camilla and Jonathon, Mila and Liam — all accounted for and healthy. And their houses are fine, too."

"So beautiful to hear. I'm dreading to see what the rest of the coastline looks like," Olivia said. "And I'm praying my house is okay."

"All that matters is we're all here. We're all still here. And we're going to get your guests back home, safe and sound. I can promise you that." Amelia paused again and then said, "Let me call over to the depot and get that started for you. I'll call you when I have more information."

"Okay." Olivia heaved a sigh. "On my end, I guess, I have about forty-seven hungry mouths to feed. And a whole lot of explaining to do."

"I can't imagine."

OLIVIA COULD HAVE KISSED her chef straight on the mouth. She discovered him already up to his elbows in breakfast preparations, his eyes dark and his brows furrowed. He instructed the other staff members on what to chop, what to mix together, how to formulate the kind of breakfast that "really got people started." When his eyes found Olivia's, he nodded firmly, like a soldier at the head of the ranks. The war was nearly over.

"Thank you," she breathed.

"Don't mention it," he replied. "I heard you on the phone in the foyer. You got a plan?"

"I spoke to Amelia. We should have some buses to get these people out of here soon," she said. "Along with the rest of us. Is your phone back on? Your people okay?"

He nodded. "Everyone is safe and accounted for."

The dining room was a funny sight. Guests slept on in various positions — strewn across couches, and huddled under blankets. These were the upper-echelon of society, the sort of ladies who never allowed the world to peer at them if their hair wasn't coordinated just so. Now, they stretched themselves up from their make-shift pillows to show hair that looked more like roadkill than anything else. If the situation hadn't been so dire, Olivia might have made time to laugh.

Olivia greeted everyone just past seven and explained the strategy at hand. First, breakfast. Second, buses to the ferry. The previous night, she and Anthony had gathered up as many items as they'd been able to muster from the rooms upstairs and delivered them out to the guests, who now had gathered their belongings around them on the ground, as though that space on the carpeting was their territory. Much of the rest had been destroyed.

Sure these people were rich. They had thick bank accounts and deep pockets. Losing items like that shouldn't have bothered them. But it still did. Of course, it did. It all contributed to a ballooning trauma.

Chelsea and Anthony stepped out from the back hallway. Chelsea stretched her thin arms over her head and yawned, her mouth stretching like a lion's. Anthony dotted a kiss on Olivia's cheek and said, "Good work on everything this morning."

"I just want to make sure everyone is okay," she told him.

The buses arrived a good twenty minutes later than they'd been scheduled, which left her guests enough room to complain their little hearts out. Olivia yearned to describe to them just what state the rest of the island was probably in, that the buses had probably had to weave and wind through several disasters in order to find them.

"Have they never had a single thing go wrong in their lives before?" Chelsea breathed into her mother's ear.

Olivia shook her head, not wanting to give in to her buzzing annoyance.

The men who owned some of the immaculate cars on the property insisted on staying behind with them to ensure they were fixed properly. Olivia explained that each of the vehicles would have to be towed and that they needed all the guests off the premises to begin the clean-up process. One of the men, the particularly aggressive one who owned the Porsche, pointed up at the gashing hole in the top of The Hesson House and said, "Clean-up process? I don't think a little vacuuming is going to fix up that place, lady."

Olivia's nostrils flared as she explained yet again. "If you want to stay on Martha's Vineyard, that's up to you. But you can't stay here." She passed several of the men her business cards and instructed them to call her in no less than three days. By then, she would have more information on their vehicles. At least, she hoped she would.

Just then, she needed them out of there.

The buses disappeared down the long drive and then chugged out toward Oak Bluffs. Olivia's shoulders shook with apprehension. It was time to face the music, to face the destruction and devastation of what the storm left behind, without the fluff of dealing with the tourists. Olivia slowly turned back to see it in all its glory: the house that had changed her life forever.

Anthony smacked his palms together. "Not a whole lot we can do before the rest of the water clears out."

Olivia nodded. "True."

"I think it's best that we try to get back to your house. Clean up a little bit. Get some more food in our systems. Maybe have a real sleep."

Olivia nodded again. She felt as though she would have

nodded to anything. She'd had to grapple with so many decisions over the previous twenty-four hours, and she wasn't sure she could ever make another again. Anthony slipped his fingers through hers and focused his eyes on her face. Still, she couldn't move her gaze from that gash in the top window, the way the walls had caved out in the bottom floor, and the way the water ran itself around the mansion.

"How are we going to get home?" Olivia asked gently.

Suddenly, dock-worker Tony appeared through the trees. He waved a hand and hollered that his truck still worked. "Thank goodness, huh?" he said as he jangled his keys. "I just bought that baby last year." He said he'd be happy to bring them back to Edgartown. His eyes flashed toward Chelsea excitedly, as though he'd ensured his truck had avoided storm damage just for her, to ensure she would be safe. Chelsea grumbled inwardly but then feigned a smile— the kind men like Tony weren't accustomed to.

"That's so great, Tony. Thank you."

They gathered the things they needed and then jumped into Tony's truck. From the rearview mirror, Tony had hung a stuffed animal, which he announced he'd won from the Oak Bluffs festival that summer. "I want to give it to my kid, but his mom took him to Boston," he said. "And what's more, she recently told me I might not be the father! So, maybe I should keep the little teddy for myself?"

"I think you should still give it to the child," Olivia said. "What are you going to do with a little bear?"

Tony looked at the bear doubtfully, then turned the engine on. "There she goes! All right. Let's get out of here."

The truck eased down the long driveway, careful to miss the

strewn limbs and ragged logs from the trees on either side. Olivia gripped Chelsea's hand and found her gaze.

"Have you gotten cell service back?" she asked.

"Yes," Chelsea affirmed.

"Any word from your father? Or Xavier?"

Chelsea just shrugged. This was clearly a topic of conversation she wanted to push off for another day.

Tony weaved the truck out onto the main road and headed southward toward Edgartown. Only a few other vehicles were out. Toward the coastline, water had drawn itself up over the tree lines and gurgled toward the road, threatening to press toward their wheels. A smaller house nearer the coast had been half-obliterated. Olivia hadn't any idea who had once lived there; she prayed they'd found relief.

Olivia's house on Captain's Walk was a few blocks from the upper part of Katama Bay. She squeezed Chelsea's hand harder as they approached. Toward the south-eastern part of Captain's Walk, water glimmered, but their little Mecca of land was safe, with just little trickles of water oozing around it. Olivia and Chelsea leaped from Tony's truck and hustled inside, where they discovered nearly everything intact. Only a single window on the eastern side had smashed through. It seemed that a tree branch had been thrown across the yard. It now hung strangely between shards of glass and fluttered in the breeze.

Olivia wrapped her arms around her daughter and held her there in the bathroom, alongside that branch as it swayed to-and-fro in the wind. Tears sped down her cheeks and stained the shoulders of Chelsea's sweatshirt. This was the first time Olivia had allowed herself to fully weep.

When she pulled back, she found that Chelsea, too, had begun to cry. Olivia wrapped one of Chelsea's rogue curls around her ear and whispered, "We're going to be okay, honey. Everything is okay."

Chelsea nodded, although her eyes told a far different story.

Anthony appeared in the hallway. He ran his fingers through his hair and said, "Chels? Tony says he won't get out of here until he gets to tell you goodbye."

Chelsea turned and cast Anthony one of those horrifically pointed, dark gazes. She glared at him with more severity and power than Olivia had seen in years. After just a moment, Anthony flung his palms skyward and said, "Okay. I'll get him out of here. I promise."

When Anthony disappeared again to get rid of Tony, Chelsea's tears mixed with laughter, and Olivia joined in. Chelsea's head found her mother's chest as she exhaled, exhausted.

"I knew I always liked him, Mom. You picked good."

"I really did. And maybe that's all I was meant to get out of The Hesson House, anyway."

Chelsea lifted her head gingerly. "What do you mean?"

"I mean, the place is so messed up, Chels. I have no idea what will happen next."

"But that doesn't mean you're going to give up on it. It's been your dream all year long."

Olivia nodded, even as her heart thudded with dread. "All I want, right now, is to sleep. Let's talk about the rest later."

CHAPTER TWELVE

OLIVIA AND CHELSEA perched at the edge of the couch, both in worn t-shirts and torn shorts. They balanced cereal bowls filled with Cinnamon Toast Crunch on their laps and leaned toward the television, which had only just come back on after three days of no-power. On-screen, a freelance cameraman, named Henry showed his footage of the devastation that had overtaken the island three days previously of demolished houses, splintered trees, and how extensive the flooding had gotten.

"There's the school!" Olivia cried as the image of the hallway between the history and the math classrooms appeared, rushing with water. "Goodness, look at that."

"How long did they say it would be until school came back?"

"We should be back in session next week," Olivia affirmed. "They have a pretty good system in place. And this footage? Ah, yeah. It says it's from the day after. I bet that's all clear now."

The images continued: the busted windows at the Sunrise

Cove Inn, along with a small portion of the Sunrise Cove Bistro, which had been smashed through with a nearby tree. Then, there was the Katama Lodge and Wellness Spa, which had a bit of flooding in the bottom floor but had more or less made it out okay. Olivia half-remembered that this filmmaker, Henry, actually dated Janine Grimson — although she couldn't fully be sure. This was a question for Jennifer at a later date.

Then, Henry weaved his camera toward The Hesson House. The water had receded since that first day and a strange, almost sinister sunlight allowed the camera to catch every peak in the once glorious building, every hole, every shattered bit of glass. The filmmaker spoke over the images and said, "This beautiful, old-world mansion took a real hit during Hurricane Janine, which as we know, was now a relatively low-grade hurricane — one that eventually went on to hit the North and South Carolinas much harder than it hit us. The Hesson House only just opened in July — to tremendous acclaim and success. Unfortunately, nature had a far different idea in mind for the future of The Hesson House."

Olivia turned her eyes toward her cereal bowl. The milk soured and curled around the little morsels of sugar and spice. Chelsea gripped the remote and clicked off the television.

After a long, tense pause, Olivia said the words that she seemed to continue to return to: "I'm still so glad you're here, Chels. But you know, you can head back to the city any time you like. I don't want to keep you from your work."

Chelsea collected Olivia's bowl and walked slowly toward the kitchen. The air stretched thin with her lack of an answer. She turned on the water which had blissfully come on along with the electricity, and washed the bowls, then tapped them gently in the drying rack. Both knew it was nearly time to head to The Hesson House, anyway. Olivia had hired someone to come out and assess the damage from a monetary perspective.

Ultimately, the assessor would give her the final word: would The Hesson House live? Or would it die?

Olivia and Chelsea separated to clean themselves up. In the shower, Olivia's fingernails scrubbed a bit too hard on her scalp. Her mind flip-flopped between different fears: what the heck had happened between Chelsea and Tyler? Was she speaking to Xavier? And what would happen if the assessor named a cost so excruciatingly high, it sent her out of The Hesson House for good? By the time she cut off the water, she'd worked herself into a tizzy. She exhaled and placed her hand in the fog of the glass and formed a perfect handprint.

Anthony had spent the morning at The Hesson House, clearing out brush and sweeping up glass and ensuring that all antique furniture was salvaged and taken to a safer location outside of the elements. Olivia and Chelsea had been up there the previous two days, doing just that. They had the scabs and scrapes and brewing callouses on their hands to prove it.

Olivia and Chelsea stopped off at the Frosted Delights en route to The Hesson House. This was the first day they'd reopened since the storm, and already, a line snaked out the door. Jennifer spotted Olivia outside the window, gathered a wide selection of donuts in a box, and headed out into the sun to greet them. Olivia and Jennifer shared a long, rib-crushing hug before Jennifer traded off for Chelsea. When their hugs broke, tears crested their cheeks.

"I don't know what to say," Jennifer said.

"We're headed there right now," Olivia affirmed. "To meet with Mr. Ralkin for the assessment."

Jennifer nodded. "I can't even imagine what you're feeling."

"Like the bubble's about to burst, I guess," Olivia replied.

"I put twelve donuts in there," Jennifer said. "I don't think anything will help you. But throwing sugar at a problem, as far as I can tell, doesn't hurt."

"You're the best, Jen."

"I'm not. But I will be murdered if I don't get back in there and help my mother," Jennifer said. "Hurricanes make people hungry. Oh, Chelsea, when do you go back to the city?"

Chelsea pressed her lips together as her cheeks burned red. "I'm not sure."

"You want to help out here. I get it," Jennifer affirmed. "Hope to see you again before you head back." She then fled back into the chaos of the bakery as Olivia and Chelsea turned back for the car.

***

ANTHONY SAT with his shoulders hunched on the front steps of The Hesson House, with the mouth of the foyer wide open behind him. It looked as though the mansion was on the verge of eating him up, swallowing him whole. It reminded Olivia of a Stephen King novel. As they parked the car, Anthony stood slowly and stretched his palm across his lower back.

"Are you hurt?" Olivia called as she stepped out of the car.

"I just pushed myself a little bit, moving an old wardrobe earlier," he said.

Olivia hustled up the steps. Chelsea carried the batch of donuts proudly. Olivia placed her hand on Anthony's lower back and breathed, "No more lifting for a while, okay?"

"We've got it all cleared out anyway," Anthony said. "Thank goodness."

"And most of it was salvageable?"

"A lot of the most expensive stuff made it through," Anthony said.

"We can maybe sell it at auction. If we have to," Olivia returned.

"Don't talk like that yet."

Olivia cast her eyes to the ground just as Mr. Ralkin's truck appeared in the driveway. Her heart pattered wildly. It was nearly the moment of reckoning.

Mr. Ralkin was quite short, no more than five foot six, and sharply dressed in a grey suit and a pair of shiny black shoes. He greeted them without warmth but with a sense of duty and brought with him a large clipboard and a pen, on which he prepared to make a series of notes about the state of the place. His eyes scanned the open mouth of the foyer and then turned upward toward more of the dilapidation. He clucked his tongue and scribed the first of what would be many notes.

"We love this place," Olivia told him, as though any amount of love could save anything at all.

Mr. Ralkin didn't have the appropriate response. Olivia wasn't sure why she wanted him to. His duty didn't involve empathy. It was all dollars and cents.

It took Mr. Ralkin no longer than an hour to go through the entire property: as far up the steps as he could, down into the basement, and around the back, where the water still poured over the tennis courts in a manner that seemed almost laughable. Nature seemed to mock them at every corner.

The number he rolled out toward the end was just as laughable. "The damages are upward of a million dollars," he said. "Perhaps more."

It was with this number in mind that Olivia poured herself what Chelsea described as "the largest glass of wine in the history of man" later that evening. Anthony had decided to grab a bite to eat with a new buddy, which had left Olivia and Chelsea to do the only thing they could think to do: invite the other Sisters of Edgartown over to the house, order a bunch of unhealthy food, and mope.

"You want one?" Olivia asked Chelsea, the bottle still poised.

"What the heck," Chelsea said. "I'm almost twenty, right?"

"You're old enough right now," Olivia affirmed as she poured her daughter a glass. "We've been through hell and back together. You can sure as heck have a glass of wine."

The other girls arrived just as four giant, cheesy pizzas arrived from the local Edgartown pizza place. Each fell upon Olivia with enormous hugs. She'd given them the number — upwards of a million — in the group text, and the shock of it had been enormous, the kind that received only text messages in return like:

WHAT THE HECK? and **IS HE SURE?**

"I'm so sorry, Liv," Camilla breathed into her ear as she rubbed her back. "I can hardly believe it."

"I haven't reached any level of acceptance yet," Olivia said as she opened the door wider for her girls.

"The first level of grief is eating pizza," Jennifer affirmed. "It's basic science."

Amelia had brought Mandy along with her. Mandy was seven months pregnant; Amelia was six, and the two of them seemed to glow with this impossible promise, something Olivia wished she could bottle and drink for breakfast.

"Sorry, I'm just about as big as a whale," Mandy said with a sneaky smile as she sat on Olivia's couch.

"You're growing a whole human inside of you. You're allowed," Chelsea told her as she wiggled in between Mandy and Amelia. "Both of you. All I've done today is eat my weight in cereal and donuts. If I become as big as a whale, it's my own fault."

Mandy chuckled and rubbed her hand over her belly. Amelia's eyes were stormy, as though her mind raced a million miles a minute.

"What's up, Amelia?" Olivia paused as she lifted a slice of pizza to her lips.

"I was just thinking. I don't know."

"Uh oh." Mila arched one of her perfect eyebrows and ogled her. "Never good when Amelia Taylor starts thinking."

"Come on," Amelia said with a sneaky smile. "I'm not that bad."

"You always have a scheme up your sleeves," Jennifer said.

"She wouldn't be my Aunt Amelia if she didn't," Mandy offered.

Amelia pressed her lips together and placed her plate off to the side, untouched.

"Amelia! This is literally the only time in your life that you can eat to your heart's content. What are you doing?" Mila joked.

But Amelia seemed hungry for a different sort of nourishment. "Did you girls see that video footage that Henry put together?"

"We watched it this morning," Chelsea affirmed.

"Yeah. I caught some of it," Jennifer said.

"The island has really hit a rough patch," Amelia noted. "And we're at the tail-end of any kind of tourist season, which means we won't exactly make the revenue back easily."

"Great. More bad news. Thanks, Amelia," Mila replied somberly.

"Let me talk!" Amelia said, feigning playfulness, even as her mind worked overtime. "I just think we should make something happen. Maybe a fundraiser. We could raise funds for The Hesson House and all others affected by the hurricane. We could have it in the next month or so. Really generate a lot of buzz and circumstance around it, so we can bring in a lot of high-rollers. We could even have some kind of auction."

"But do you really think something like this could generate upwards of a million, plus all the funds necessary for the other establishments?" Olivia asked.

Amelia shrugged. "There's no reason we can't try. And if we can't get the number up enough this round, there's no reason we can't have more down the line."

Olivia turned her eyes toward Chelsea. Intrigue had settled itself into her stomach — along with something else. Maybe there was hope.

"But Amelia, listen. You're pregnant and you just got out of bedrest only a few weeks ago," Jennifer pointed out.

"I know. But I'm feeling so much better."

"But you shouldn't push it," Olivia affirmed. "No. I won't sacrifice the health of your baby and you — all for this."

"But come on, Olivia. This is a great opportunity. And you

don't want to let The Hesson House die after only two months in operation."

Olivia heaved a sigh. Jennifer placed her plate of half-eaten pizza off to the side, clapped her hands together, and said, "There's no reason we can't all pitch in to make this happen."

"Absolutely," Camilla affirmed. "Amelia, we know you're a control freak, but is there any way you could let us carry the load?"

Amelia nodded, albeit tentatively. "Normally, I can do something like this in my sleep."

"But we don't want you to," Olivia said. "Please."

Amelia lifted her slice of pizza and took a large bite, which she chewed slowly. After a long pause, she swallowed and said, "Okay. But you have to do whatever I say when I say it. Is that a deal?"

"Oh, great. Here we go," Mila said playfully, rolling her eyes.

But in the wake of this decision, Olivia's heart lifted as though it had suddenly grown the most beautiful pair of wings.

CHAPTER THIRTEEN

FIVE DAYS SINCE THE HURRICANE. Five days since Chelsea had made her spontaneous decision to disappear from her New York life and do one of the more cowardly things she'd ever done in her life: seek out her mother and hide. Now, she lay in her childhood bed, all wrapped up in blankets, three pillows behind her, and wondered if she'd ever had the strength to return. Her heart hammered with the thought of it. She thought about reading the fifty-plus messages from both her father and Xavier. Anxiety had become like a dear friend. She carried it around on her shoulder like a parrot.

Outside her bedroom, her mother paced as she spoke on the phone with Amelia about the potential fundraiser. Chelsea groaned and shifted beneath the blankets. The alarm clock on her bedside table read 11:14 in big, bold red letters. It demanded something of her. It wondered why the heck she refused to get up. She wondered it of herself, too. Was this depression? She had certainly grappled with that as a teenager in the wake of her father's departure. She imagined telling her father that, now. "What you did to me when I was a teenager messed me up for good. And now you just show up unannounced and use me like this?'

Again, her phone began to buzz. It was Xavier. She allowed it to buzz itself until it couldn't buzz any longer. Again, Xavier left a voicemail, another in a list of eleven. They had definitely read about The Hesson House and they had probably guessed that's where she'd gone. She felt akin to a monster, having abandoned them. Then again, it was true what they said on airplanes: you had to put on your own oxygen mask before helping anyone else with theirs. In the recent weeks, she'd had great difficulty in learning how to breathe.

Chelsea slid out of bed and padded to the bathroom, where she took full stock of herself. Her reflection looked pale, a sunken-in face that had once blossomed with life and optimism. She brushed her teeth and then flossed, something she rarely did but made a mental note to do more. Life was long and unnecessarily cruel. You had to be kind to your teeth.

In the kitchen, she poured herself a mug of coffee as Olivia finally drew her conversation closed. She placed her phone on the counter then positioned her hands on her hips.

"I don't know. Do you think we can pull it off?"

"Sure," Chelsea said, not really sounding sure herself. But this was the only appropriate response.

"What are you doing today?" Olivia asked.

Chelsea knew what the question meant: it demanded much more of Chelsea than she was willing to give. She couldn't go into the details of why she had left the city, nor could she discuss the fact that she had pondered whether or not she wanted to return to the city at all. The diner had reopened in the wake of the storm. Perhaps they could just pass on a few shifts to her, here and there. She could slip back into her old life like nothing had happened.

But time didn't move in that direction. It didn't go backward.

"I don't know," Chelsea finally offered. "I feel a bit at a loss."

Olivia nodded. "Me too." She sipped her coffee, then scrunched her nose and added a hint of milk. "You know, you can talk to me about it if you want to."

This couldn't have been further from the truth. "I know," she lied.

"Are they okay?"

"Yes." Again, a lie. Chelsea felt herself moving emotionally further and further away from her mother.

Her phone buzzed with a message from Marty, her boss.

MARTY: Hey girl. Are you ready for your shift tomorrow evening?

Chelsea's heart banged away in her ribcage. She scrunched her nose and ignored it. Olivia noted this and arched an eyebrow.

"You have to get back to work?"

Chelsea nodded. "Yeah, I guess so."

"You don't want to tell him you're needed here a little while longer?"

Chelsea wasn't sure why, but she resented her mother saying this. She could "need" her mother all she liked until that very mother pointed out the fact. Chelsea shook her head so that her curls wafted across her shoulders.

"I can't lose my job, Mom." Her voice dripped with aggression.

Olivia leaned up against the counter, mug in hand. "I know that, honey."

Gosh, there was so much unsaid. It felt like a crater between them.

"I'm going to go for a run," Chelsea told her. "Clear my head a bit."

"Okay. Do you want company?"

Chelsea and Olivia used to go jogging together, back when Chelsea had experimented with the cross country team in high school. Chelsea had been impressed with her mother's ability to stretch long miles across back roads and hills, despite being twenty years her senior.

"No. I'm good."

Olivia looked shrunken. "Okay."

Chelsea donned a pair of running shorts and an old high school sweatshirt. She pushed her feet into old tennis shoes and walked out the door. Once there, she drew a line northward down Captain's Walk and headed up through Edgartown, where she passed a number of piles of rubble and debris, all collected post-hurricane. Several Edgartown residents lined the sidewalk and discussed the events. It really seemed there was no end in sight with regards to conversation topics about the storm. This was the pinnacle of gossip. It was Martha's Vineyard's top fuel. As she raced, several onlookers waved a hand in greeting. They all recognized her — Olivia Hesson's daughter, of course, the one who had run off to New York. She could practically feel the gossip swirling out from their lips regarding her. "What happened to that boyfriend of hers? He was always such a surly character. Wonder if he got her pregnant yet?"

Chelsea's nostrils flared at this imagined conversation. Wasn't this gossip the very reason she'd wanted to escape Martha's Vineyard, anyway? But no. It had been bigger than that. She had longed for so much more in life — the kind of life she'd read about in books. Chelsea had imagined that she could craft whatever existence she wanted, as long as she fought, tooth and nail for it. She hadn't imagined Tyler would just appear into that life without notice. She hadn't imagined this crash-and-burn.

She rushed all the way to the Edgartown Lighthouse, where she nearly collapsed, gripping her knees as she blinked bleary eyes across the now-calm waters. When the hurricane had rolled toward Martha's Vineyard, her heart had burned with fear that she wouldn't reach her mother in time. She had wanted to tell her something — something enormous, something she couldn't name now. Perhaps it was something along the lines of, "I'm sorry." But that now seemed too simplistic. Plus, they'd gotten through the storm, and they had returned to either side of their war lines. There was just so much Chelsea and Olivia couldn't say to one another. Too much had happened in the past.

Chelsea's phone buzzed with a call from Andrea. Andrea was Camilla's daughter, a full three years older than Chelsea — yet eternally one of Chelsea's dearest friends. Since Chelsea had moved to Brooklyn, she and Andrea had struggled to catch one another, between Andrea's difficult fashion school schedule and Chelsea's late-night restaurant shifts. Still, they met for the occasional coffee, where normally, Andrea listened as Chelsea gushed about how much she loved the city. Chelsea kept any of her "homesickness" woes to herself, as she didn't want Andrea to think she was weak.

"Hey," Chelsea answered as brightly as she could.

"Chels, hi." Andrea's voice was pinched. "You're not in the city."

"No. I'm not." Chelsea drew upright and walked slowly along the boardwalk. Much of the railing had been obliterated; little twigs and stones lined the walkway. Probably, the bigger debris had already been moved away.

"I just ran into Xavier," Andrea said.

Chelsea's heart sank into her stomach. She allowed the silence to sink between them.

"He looked bad, Chels. Like, worse than I've ever seen him."

Chelsea wanted to point out that Andrea didn't know Xavier that well. She was three years older than Chelsea in school and thusly four years older than Xavier. They'd interacted over the summer at bonfires and parties and stuff, but that was about it.

"Why did you leave, Chelsea? I couldn't get it out of him. Last time I saw you, you were all, 'New York is my home forever.'"

Chelsea buzzed her lips. "I didn't realize I was in for a huge interrogation today."

"So you're on the Vineyard?"

"Yes, detective. I'm on the island of Martha's Vineyard."

"Don't be like that."

"Like what?" Chelsea placed her hand on her hips as she felt her sarcasm sizzle across her tongue.

"You know like what. Chelsea, I'm not your enemy here. But you should have told me. I said that I'd watch out for you in the city."

"You're so busy with school. And I don't need to be 'watched out for.' I'm not a kid."

"Chelsea. Are you going to come back? Are you going to tell Xavier what's up?"

Chelsea swallowed the lump in her throat. Every cell in her body screamed with the desire to see Xavier again, to feel his strong arms around her as they slept through the night as the city's wheels spun around them, a non-stop, whirling ecosystem of madness.

"My dad came to the city."

"What? Tyler?"

Chelsea sniffed. "Xavier got so mad at me for letting him stay with us. And to be honest, I'm angry with him, too. I love my dad so much. You know I do. But he crossed every line. And I couldn't stop him. So I ran here and I wound up center-stage in line for the storm of a lifetime."

"You and Tyler both have excellent timing," Andrea returned.

"Gee. Thanks."

Andrea sighed. "I want to talk more, but I have a class in a few minutes. Will you call me later?"

Chelsea pressed her eye hard with two fingers; light yellow spots formed behind her eyelid.

"I don't know, Andrea. I don't know what to do with myself."

"You'll get through this, Chelsea. You will. You're strong."

"I don't feel very strong."

"Come on. You're a queen. Don't make me tell you again."

They hung up the phone. Chelsea pressed her phone against her chest and pondered what to do next. In some respects, her bed back at home screamed louder than ever. She yearned to crawl beneath those covers, pop on a Netflix show, and continue hiding from the world for the rest of her days. Olivia would allow it for a while. Heck, she'd sit with her in bed without prying and cook them delicious snacks.

But Chelsea knew in her heart this sort of hiding-out was similar to a prison. It was a prison of perception. She would be allowed only the safety of this previous world while dismissing the one she truly belonged in.

Still, saying that to herself felt very different than living it.

When Chelsea announced her plans to return to the city the following morning, Olivia pressed her lips into a thin, pale line. Her eyes brewed with questions. Before her was a fifteen-point to-do list, presumably for the upcoming fundraiser; her hand shook over the paper as she collected her thoughts.

"Are you sure you want to go back?"

Chelsea bristled. "Yes. I'm sure."

Olivia dropped her pen. She looked to toss Chelsea question after question, like darts thrown at a board in a dive bar.

But instead, Olivia just nodded. "I know you know what you're doing. I know you know how to handle yourself."

Chelsea balked. Had Olivia Hesson been taken? Was this an alien life force, speaking through the body of her mother?

Chelsea hadn't fully realized how much she'd wanted her mother to protest her decision until she didn't. This was a funny thing about human nature. We always want the opposite of what we have. Why is that? Chelsea wondered now.

"Cool. Well. I'll just be in my room, then."

"Great. I'll order a pizza for your last night," Olivia told her with a smile. "And I'll crack a bottle of wine. Cabernet good for you?"

CHAPTER FOURTEEN

MARTY'S TEXT arrived just as Chelsea disembarked to the subway platform nearest her apartment in Brooklyn.

MARTY: Glad to have you back on staff tonight.

MARTY: But no more running off like that. Or else! LOL.

Chelsea grumbled and shoved her phone back into her pocket. Apparently, Xavier's showing up at the restaurant the previous week had alerted Marty of her lie about being sick. Good thing Marty seemed to like her — even if that "liking" was suspect. She needed the job.

The smells of the city hit her differently as she sauntered down the sidewalk. Swirls of urine and slices of cheesy pizza and smog, all of it assaulted her nostrils, especially after six days on Martha's Vineyard — that pinnacle of glorious salty sea scents and, of course, the comfortable smells of home.

Chelsea hadn't told Xavier about her plans to return home. She hadn't a single idea of what she would find once she snuck her key in the lock and twisted the door to that dank little apartment. Perhaps her father would still be collapsed on the sofa; perhaps Xavier would be a moody shadow of horror in their bedroom. Perhaps Xavier would take one look at her and demand a break-up, or Tyler would look at her and not even remember that she'd been gone for six full days. Time was different for everyone; she knew this. She felt as though she had lived a small infinity on the Vineyard, with the hurricane, the subsequent collapse and her non-stop thoughts, which had swirled deep into the night.

She had lived an entire lifetime without the two of them. But what had they done in the interim?

There it was: her key. It flashed up from her pocket, and she poised it in the little mouth of the door. This was the moment of truth. After a deep breath, she pushed it in and drew open the door. That near-mold smell curled into her nostrils. And bit by bit, she caught more and more of the scene of the apartment—a space for all intents and purposes, seemed rather clean, perhaps cleaner than it had been six days before. All the dishes were set up in the little make-shift cabinet; the counters were wiped down; and the couch was just two barren cushions, without a rogue dad at all. In fact, nothing of Tyler came into view throughout this initial analysis.

"Hello?" Chelsea's voice brimmed with curiosity.

Xavier appeared in the doorway between the kitchen and the bedroom. He scrubbed his eyes sleepily and peered at her as though she was a figment in a dream.

It was true what Andrea had said: Xavier did look rough. His skin was pale, and he'd lost a bit of weight, so much that his ribcage poked out just a little. His cheeks were hollow, and his hair was scruffy and wild, the way it was when he didn't shower. Chelsea's arms shook with sorrow. She kicked the door closed behind her and hustled up to him. Her arms wrapped around him tenderly, and she placed her head against his chest. For a long time, during their embrace, she felt that she would never find the strength to ask him if he was all right. She had him here; she would help care for him, now. It couldn't be the other way around, non-stop, any longer.

A few minutes later, Chelsea placed a bag of microwave popcorn in the microwave and gathered several blankets, which she wrapped around them both on the couch. They held hands and listened as the microwave popcorn bag gave in to the heat around it and bubbled up into the perfect, buttery snack. Chelsea leaped up to grab it, then watched as Xavier plopped three puffs on his tongue and closed his eyes.

"Good, huh?" Chelsea said.

"I've had popcorn before, Chels."

"Yeah? Because it looks like you haven't eaten anything at all in the last week."

Xavier's shoulders dropped forward. Chelsea immediately regretted her words. She slid a hand over his back and whispered, "Come on. I didn't mean it. I'm sorry."

"No. You're right. I kind of broke down."

Chelsea bit hard on her tongue. After a long pause, she said, "I'm so sorry I didn't read your messages. Or answer your calls."

Xavier's eyes were firm. "Don't do that to me again, Chelsea."

Chelsea understood. This was a line in the sand. If she crossed this boundary, Xavier would probably find it very difficult to forgive her again. People had to build their own boundaries. Chelsea knew this, especially since she'd never been able to draw her own regarding her father.

"What happened?" Chelsea said finally. She tapped the empty couch.

Xavier swallowed more popcorn. His eyes found the ground. "We were both freaked that you left like that. And I might have said a few choice words about him coming here and about him cornering you like that."

Chelsea couldn't blame Xavier. She just hated herself for making him fight her battles for her.

"What did he say?"

"Well. That's where it gets interesting."

Chelsea's eyes widened in anticipation.

"He became silent, then agreed with me. He had tears in eyes, Chelsea," Xavier affirmed.

"No!"

Xavier nodded.

"What did you do?"

"I didn't know what to do. So I suggested we go get something to eat. It was awkward, but we both ate and he acknowledged his mistakes. He admitted that he really messed up and didn't know what to do and thought of you. I also had to remind him that you're his daughter, not his therapist and that it wasn't cool."

Chelsea couldn't help but chuckle. "Oh my God. It sounds awful."

"It was. In a sad, funny way."

"Essentially, he regrets... everything. Everything in his life," Xavier continued. "He hates that he left you and Olivia. He hates now that he can't fully handle his girlfriend having a baby. And he hates that he didn't treat her right. He wanted to go back bad."

"Is that where he is now?"

"I don't actually know," Xavier returned. "I don't want to freak you out, but after that dinner, I think Tyler was too embarrassed to stay here. He packed up and headed out. We don't have each other's numbers or anything, so. Yeah. That's the last I know."

Chelsea placed her head tenderly on Xavier's shoulder. She didn't have any words. It all felt so tremendously heavy — from this story to the one over on the Vineyard of The Hesson House and its potential closure that could last forever. She explained this to Xavier, the fear she'd had as she had hustled into The Hesson House as the hurricane had hit.

"I was freaked out, to put it lightly," Xavier explained. "I figured you went home. And then, it was all the news could talk about for a few days. What was up on Martha's Vineyard? I saw it everywhere. And at first, my calls and texts weren't going through. When they did, you weren't answering them. And —"

"I know. It was awful of me. I know."

Xavier buzzed his lips. "I won't dwell."

Chelsea lifted her chin and met his gaze. "You know that I love you, right?"

"I love you, too."

Chelsea kissed him softly, then stood and texted her father.

CHELSEA: I don't want to know anything else. I just want to make sure you're okay.

Only a moment later, Tyler got back with her.

DAD: I'm okay.

Chelsea sniffed, shoved her phone into her pocket, and then

whirled around to ask, "Do you want to go explore for a while? I don't have to be at work till seven-thirty. And I am dying for one of our classic New York adventures."

Xavier showered — something he confessed he hadn't done in a number of days. Chelsea then willed him to write his work to tell them he'd be back in the following day. They then dressed against the chill of the late-September early afternoon and stepped out into the streets of Brooklyn. Chelsea's heart lifted as Xavier slipped his fingers through hers. They were two pieces of the same puzzle. She couldn't believe she had nearly allowed herself to forget.

They took the subway into Manhattan. Once there, they followed the streets up, all the way to Central Park. Late September meant crisp orange and brown leaves, which played out a beautiful contrast to the still-green grass below. The blue sky was a perfect crescent over them, cocooning them and all the city below. They passed people from all walks of life: a family from India, with two little girls dressed up in Disney princess dresses, hopping around as their mother attempted to make them sit to eat their packed picnic. Beyond them, a cyclist stopped short as a big dog, one that looked like Lassie, hustled off to fetch a ball. As they continued on, they heard the beautiful strum of a guitar. And when they reached the same fountain where the opening credits of the TV show Friends was filmed — they discovered him. A guitarist with a microphone was singing that old Frank Sinatra song, "New York, New York."

"It feels like the last scene in a movie," Xavier joked.

"Yeah, the one with Meg Ryan in it," Chelsea agreed as she dropped her head onto his chest.

"I wonder what would happen now? In the movie? While the two main characters watch the guitarist?"

"I don't know," Chelsea returned softly.

"Probably they would kiss right here in front of everyone."

Chelsea lifted her chin with a smile. "If you insist."

Xavier had never been a particularly romantic guy when she had first met him. According to her mother, who had been his English teacher at the time, Xavier had been incredibly troubled, a dark and brooding soul on the brink of some kind of mental collapse. But as he kissed her there in front of the busker in Central Park, she felt the wealth and bounty and beauty of his soul. She knew they would be all right, as long as they were together.

When their kiss broke, she whispered, "You're just one big softie, aren't you, Xavier?"

"When it comes to you, I guess I am," Xavier returned. "And — about your dad…"

"I know. I know. I give him every chance in the world," Chelsea said. "But I'm done with that."

"It's not that, exactly. It's just that I know it's been hard for you. And I know you love him, which makes it just that much worse. But fathers can't always be what we need them to be, which is why I want to tell you, here and now, in front of this cheesy busker in Central Park that I will be there for you in everything, every day — for as long as you'll let me."

"For as long as you'll let me, I'll be there for you, too." Chelsea's throat thickened as tears welled in her eyes.

For a nineteen and an eighteen-year-old, these words seemed similar to wedding vows. They kissed again, then fell into one another's arms as the busker switched songs, from Sinatra to Green Day — a switch that made Xavier groan.

"All right. All right. Let's get back home," Chelsea said with a wild laugh. "I don't want you to complain so much. You ruin the music for everyone else."

Perhaps all would be well. Perhaps she hadn't made too much damage. Perhaps their mission — to craft a new life for themselves in the city could continue. And perhaps her mother had been right: she could, truly, handle anything.

CHAPTER FIFTEEN

DESPITE ALL THEIR BEST INTENTIONS, Amelia flung herself into the idea of a Hurricane Fundraiser with endless zeal. Jennifer, Olivia, Mila, and Camilla exchanged glances at their next meeting as Amelia talked quickly, her words tumbling into one another as though she had forgotten the concept of oxygen. When she finally did pause and blink up, her pen poised over her yellow pad of paper, she balked and said, "Well? What do you think?"

"I think it sounds generally good," Olivia finally offered, forcing herself forward. "But you seem — hmm."

"I seem what?" Amelia demanded.

"Really into this," Jennifer tried.

"Exhausted?" Camilla tried.

"No. No. I'm not." Amelia drew her hair behind her ear, suddenly exasperated. "I just know that the grunt work has to happen now so that we can reveal all our best-laid plans at the town meeting this weekend. If you tell the people the best strategy, they'll go along with it without hesitation. If you go in there with wishy-washy plans, then they're apt to walk all over you."

"Nobody will walk all over you," Mila tried.

But Amelia cast her a dark look, one that meant business. Mila placed a potato chip on her tongue and chewed slowly as her gaze fell to the floor. They knew better than to prod the beast — especially now, in her pregnant state.

The town meeting was set to begin at five in the evening that Saturday at the downtown assembly hall, which had enough benches and chairs to suit five hundred guests. Amelia wanted to ensure all business owners who wanted to be involved, along with everyone who had been directly affected by the hurricane, could attend. The logistics were tricky, especially as the island remained heavily in hurricane clean-up mode. The mood across the island was grim. It was as though a general cloud of despair had been cast over all of them. The fact that summer had officially dug her head into the sea didn't help matters, either. They were headed fast and hard toward the darkness, toward winter — and their island had threatened to crumble beneath them.

Olivia hugged each of her girls as they headed out into the night. Amelia assured her yet again that all would be well. "We'll get your funds for The Hesson House, honey. Mark my words." But Olivia knew better than to get her hopes up. "See you this Saturday."

Anthony wouldn't arrive back from his buddy's place for the next hour or so, which left Olivia at home on Captain's Walk. She sat on the couch and flicked through various reality TV channels as though one of them — the house-flippers or the adopters or the overseas fiancés — had any sort of answer for her desolate state. She checked her phone for the zillionth time that day, praying for an answer from Chelsea. But in the wake of her return to the city, she'd received only a few text messages here and there. She had mentioned — in a three-word text message that just read, "Dad is gone," that Tyler had departed. But where had he gone? And why had he come in the first place? Worry permeated through everything else. But Olivia reminded herself of the strength it had taken in the first place when she had told Chelsea she had it in herself to handle it. She had to stick to that sentiment. She felt it had given Chelsea a kind of courage.

If you had courage, there weren't a whole lot of boundaries in your path in this life. Olivia knew this, especially because it had taken her years to build up any kind of courage herself.

That Friday, Olivia arrived at school thirty minutes early. She placed her lunchbox in the fridge in the teacher's lounge and then turned to find Janet Maxwell, whom she'd managed to avoid in the wake of the hurricane. Now, she clucked her tongue and delivered a horrible gaze, one that was meant to transmit pity, maybe, but ultimately made Olivia feel very small.

"It's just awful what happened to that hotel of yours."

Olivia tried on a smile that ultimately failed. "Thanks. I know. Did you make it out okay with the hurricane?"

"Oh, sure. We're good. Thank goodness. It just broke my heart afterward to walk through town and see everything all mangled. But I guess that's the risk we all take, living out here on this island like we do."

"My family's been here for generations. I can't imagine ever going anywhere else," Olivia stated.

"Well, anyway." Janet seemed not to care about this sentiment at all. "At least now, you can get back to what really matters. Those students need your TLC, don't you think?"

Olivia had thrown herself almost completely into her teaching work in the wake of the hurricane. She had graded every paper ahead of time; she'd read and re-read their assignments to mentally prepare herself for discussion; and she'd come up with interesting new writing topics for several of her classes, who had taken to the material with enthusiasm.

Still, something about it all felt so empty to her. She had been a teacher for twenty years. It had been enough before. What was wrong with her? Why did she now look out on her sea of students and feel lackluster? It wasn't the students, per se. Rather, it was a shift within her own soul.

During the first period, two of her students started an argument about Gatsby's "Daisy" and whether or not she was a sympathetic character. In normal circumstances, Olivia might have relished this conversation, but in the wake of everything that had happened, her mind was elsewhere. She pushed herself to fall into it, though. She even divided the classroom up into two sides to operate the argument like a sort of makeshift courtroom. But as their points flew back and forth, her heart dipped lower into her stomach. All she could think about, no matter the date nor time, was The Hesson House. It felt like a dead thing she'd had to leave behind on the road to somewhere else.

AT FOUR-FORTY-FIVE ON SATURDAY EVENING, the assembly hall in Edgartown was a buzzing ecosystem of life and friendship and community. Olivia and Anthony entered and found themselves immediately accosted with, "Hey! Good evening!" and welcome smiles. Amelia beckoned for them to come up to a little table she'd set up, where they had to sign their names and whether or not they wanted assistance for their business or household from the funds they would generate at the hurricane fundraiser.

"Sign this girl up," Camilla said brightly as she and Jonathon eased in from the crowd off to the right.

Olivia chuckled as she penned her and Anthony's name across the pad of paper. "Yeah, I would say we need help."

"That's putting it lightly." This came from the left, from a towering force of a man, Wesley Sheridan, who owned the Sunrise Cove Inn. He smiled at Olivia warmly, like a father might, and said, "It's just awful what happened to your hotel, Olivia. My girls and I haven't been able to comprehend what you must be going through. If anything like that happened to our Sunrise Cove, I don't know what we'd do."

Olivia thanked him and stepped to the side to allow others to sign their names. "I heard the bistro got hit a little bit?"

"Not so bad," Wes affirmed. "And we probably won't take funds from the fundraiser. We'll take a little pause from the bistro, fix it back up to its original state, and then continue on. To be honest with you, it's for the best, since Christine and Zach — my daughter and her boyfriend, who run the bistro together have started to raise my granddaughter's baby, Max, while she's away at Penn State. And what's more, Christine, herself is getting bigger and bigger by the day." He wagged his eyebrows. "Another baby in the family! I feel just giddy about it. It's so wonderful."

Susan Sheridan marched up alongside her father and greeted Olivia warmly. "Is he bragging about all his grandchildren again?"

"He is. You caught him." Olivia beamed at the duo.

"Dad, not everyone wants to hear about our family tree everywhere we go," Susan teased. She then made a serious face and said, "I really was so sorry to hear about The Hesson House, Olivia. Luckily, you have Amelia Taylor in your corner."

"That's putting it lightly," Olivia affirmed.

Susan waved a hand and beckoned to another woman, Nancy Remington, the widow of Neal Remington, who had taken over the Katama Lodge and Wellness Spa after his rather sudden death the winter before. She furrowed her brow and linked a hand around Olivia's shoulder.

"Darling, it is just so awful what happened to you," Nancy breathed.

The amount of love that brewed up from the heart of Martha's Vineyard hospitality sector was unmatched. Tears sprung to Olivia's eyes. Before she could figure out what to say, besides a few fumbled, "Thank you's" Amelia announced that it was time for the town meeting to begin. Olivia and Anthony weaved down the lines of chairs to grab two seats off to the right, near the front.

"Good evening, everyone," Amelia said. Her stomach bulged out and gave her an air of strength over the rest of them. What kind of woman could arrange such an enormous island-wide function and grow a baby inside of her, all at once? That kind of woman could.

"Thank you all for coming today. Hurricane Janine ripped through the island a week and a half ago. She certainly left a lot of devastation in the wake of her path. But it's up to us to be there for one another and ensure that our island's prosperous time continues. For this reason, I would like to propose a fundraiser, to be held at the Harbor View Hotel. The grounds are enormous, and if the weather's anything like other years, we should have some beautiful blue-skied days in October, perfect for something like this."

There were murmurs across the wide expanse of islanders. Several hands stuck into the air and waved around. Amelia looked slightly annoyed, but she selected several of the community members to speak.

"My hardware store lost half of its roof," a man said off to the left. "Will I qualify for assistance?"

"Well, before we get into all the nitty-gritty details, I think it's important that you all ask your insurance providers how much they can assist you," Amelia suggested — speaking as though she spoke to a young adult.

The man sat and scratched his head as though this thought hadn't crossed his mind. Several other people stood with similar questions; others seemed on the hunt for free funds, regardless of their hurricane situation. Amelia rolled her eyes and then clapped her hands together in an attempt to silence the room so she could continue.

"Let's move on to the task at hand, shall we?" she stated loud and clear. "Later on, it will be decided if you qualify for any funds that we raise at this event."

"Who will do the deciding?" This was the hardware store man all over again.

"We have a twelve-person board that will make this assessment," Amelia affirmed. "They're life-long islanders, with a commitment to the economic ecosystem of this island. Essentially we will assess who got hit with the most damage and go from there."

The questions continued. Amelia grew increasingly exasperated. One older woman just stood up and listed all of the items in her vegetable garden that were destroyed in the hurricane. Amelia said she was sorry, but she wasn't sure the fundraiser could help her with something like that. The woman grumbled, gathered her things, and immediately left. Olivia sniggered as Anthony stabbed an elbow into her side.

"Don't laugh," Anthony breathed. "We don't want them to turn on us."

Olivia righted her face, even as a seemingly very wealthy sailing type raised a hand and said that he didn't believe it was up to the government to arrange any kind of fundraiser like this.

"Then what would you have us do?" Amelia asked him, balking.

The man wasn't sure. He returned to his seat and muttered something to his wife, clearly annoyed.

"In any case, let's continue on with the meeting. Shall we?" Amelia no longer looked particularly thrilled with her decision to handle this meeting on her own.

Slowly but surely, they nailed down the facts, which included what kinds of games they would hold, what sorts of food kiosks they would offer, and how many items they would require at auction to ensure that they generated the number of funds they required. Ultimately, the meeting was rather prosperous. And when it finished, Wes Sheridan's sister stood on a chair and hollered that she and a few of her friends had made enough clam chowder to feed an entire continent.

"I hope you will all stay for dinner and communion," she announced as she clasped her hands together, grinning from ear to ear. "And let's give a warm hand of thanks to Amelia. We don't know what we'd do without you. Please don't pull all your hair out as you deal with us."

Amelia grinned and bowed her head as rolls of applause fell over her. Olivia's heart swelled with pride. Despite wildly different personalities and countless perspectives, the island really would find a way to come together in the wake of this disaster. Naturally, coming together also meant eating to their hearts' content. This was just the Vineyard way.

CHAPTER SIXTEEN

CHELSEA'S RESTAURANT apron bulged with bills. It was just past one-thirty in the morning, and she drew open the little pouch and flicked out bill after bill, counting herself into the three-hundreds of cash-tips. Marty walked up behind her, and she rushed to put her bills away. She felt protective of her hard-earned tips. But Marty just clucked his tongue, laughing at her.

"I make way more money than you. Don't worry," he said snidely.

Chelsea yearned to roll her eyes into the back of her head. She kept her bills tucked safe and turned to meet Marty's gaze. "It's always nice to end a hard shift with one of your classic brags, Marty."

Marty's smile was electric. It showed several yellow teeth tucked behind his brighter white ones — the ones he hit hard with the toothbrush, probably. "You want a drink before you go?"

"I told you, Marty. I'm only nineteen. You could get written up."

Marty gestured out across the bar, where the bartender scrubbed the counter and another employee mopped between the tables. "Who's going to write me up, exactly?"

"I have to go," Chelsea said. "Maybe another time?"

"Another time. It's always another time with you."

Chelsea ducked out from where he'd blocked her against the wall, grabbed her coat from the hanger, and flung it over her shoulders. Men like Marty were a dime a dozen in New York. They were nothing but creepy dudes who'd never gotten what they'd truly wanted in life, so they had to intimidate you into doing whatever they pleased. Chelsea had already decided she wouldn't be that kind of girl. She needed the job, but only until she found something better— something that suited her. Something that didn't have a seven-thirty p.m. to a one-thirty time slot.

"I'll see you tomorrow, Marty," Chelsea said, her voice a mixture of sarcasm and syrupy sweetness. "Always a pleasure."

She could feel Marty's eyes burn into her back as she sauntered away. En route to the front door, she locked eyes with the bartender, who shared her eye roll. Already, she had built up a sort of rapport with many of the staff members and servers. She was widely known as a hard-ass, a woman who demanded what she wanted of the world and stood up for herself. It was only sometimes, in the quiet moments of herself as she rushed from Manhattan back to Brooklyn, that she found herself stirring in any sort of self-doubt.

But self-doubt was the name of the game. "Fake it till you make it" was the other one.

Chelsea was surprised to find Xavier at the top of the steps of the subway station when she arrived back in Brooklyn. It was a chilly late-night in late September; she'd expected him to be tucked away in bed. When he spotted her, he threw his arms around her and greeted her with warm lips and closed eyes. They kissed at the top of the steps as the city buzzed around them, a chaotic symphony of lights and blaring sirens.

"What was that for?" she asked when their kiss broke.

"Andrea told me about a party. Do you want to go?"

Chelsea laughed and tossed her head back as her hair wafted across the top of her back. "Are you serious? It looks like we're official New Yorkers and all, considering we've been invited to our first party. Very cool!"

"I knew you would like it."

"But it's later than two in the morning!"

"I know. We're in the city that never sleeps," Xavier reminded her.

"Okay. Now it feels like a challenge," Chelsea said.

They strode quickly down the block; their feet marked time toward Andrea's stated destination. When they arrived on the other side of the door, Xavier rapped his knuckles just once before a random stranger, presumably someone who didn't live at the apartment, yanked open the door and hooted in greeting.

The apartment was packed with wall-to-wall attractive and trendy people, all from Brooklyn. Chelsea slipped off her shoes near the door and piled them alongside the others. She then spotted Andrea in the corner, alongside her fiancé, Isaac, who normally lived on the island but frequently visited Andrea in the city.

Andrea leaped from the couch and wrapped her arms around Chelsea and shook her almost violently, back and forth.

"Oh my God!" she cried.

"You're going to give me whiplash," Chelsea squealed with delight as they parted.

"I was so worried about you! And now you're back and all is well!" Andrea's eyes glittered.

Xavier stepped up alongside Chelsea and passed her a beer. Chelsea exhaled deeply and then took a sip. "Whose party is this?"

"My friend Monica, from fashion school," Andrea explained. She then lowered her voice and added, "Her parents are rich as they get, so she's basically bound to be a famous fashion designer."

"That's rough," Chelsea said. "Do you like the stuff she makes?"

Andrea's eyes flashed from side to side to check for eavesdroppers. "I mean, it's not bad, exactly."

"Andrea!"

"What? You know I'm picky."

"Then I'm guessing you're not particularly into my outfit tonight? I call it waitress chic."

"You know I always think you look stunning," Andrea said, beaming. "Oh! I wanted to ask you something." She gripped Chelsea's hand drunkenly and tugged her down alongside her. "And you can say no if you want to."

"What?" Chelsea arched her brow. "You're freaking me out. Do you need a new kidney?"

"No! Idiot." Andrea flashed her blonde hair behind her shoulders and cleared her throat.

"Why do you look like you're about to announce your decision to run for president?" Chelsea asked.

"You really can't take anything seriously, can you?"

In the corner, a twenty-something kid flung himself forward and nearly vomited into a plant. His friend grabbed his elbow and guided him toward the bathroom. Xavier and Isaac began to discuss a book of poetry Xavier had recently read. Well, Xavier discussed it, while Isaac kind of passively nodded along. Chelsea sort of adored this about Xavier: he didn't care if you weren't interested in something. If he loved it, he brought it into the conversation. He never hid to suit anyone else's needs.

"Okay. Drumroll, please," Andrea said with a wide smile.

"You're so dramatic. You're perfect for the fashion world," Chelsea returned.

"Come on. Just let me have this."

Chelsea sipped her beer, cleared her throat, and finally offered a, "Ugh, fine."

"I want you to be my maid of honor. Pretty please."

Chelsea gazed into those beautiful bright blue eyes. Within them, she felt a wild collection of memories — long-ago days when their mothers had gathered together over glasses of wine while their children had scampered out across the grass and over the sands, forming new stories together, falling in love in new ways.

"Are you serious?" Chelsea asked with wide eyes.

"Are you kidding? Who else would I ask?"

"I don't know. Monica?" Chelsea joked.

"Come on, Chels. Just tell me you'll be there for me when I walk down the aisle," Andrea begged. "I seriously can't imagine anyone else taking that spot. And I know you don't fully believe in marriage and all that, but I really want it to be you."

"Who says I don't believe in marriage?" Chelsea asked.

Andrea rolled her eyes. "Only you. Like every day since, well."

"Since my dad left."

"Yeah."

Chelsea vaguely remembered those volatile words. She blinked several times at the emotional density of Andrea's question. "I'm not as much of a hard-hearted person these days, unfortunately," Chelsea told her as a grin snaked its way to her lips. "Still snarky as ever, sure. But, you know. Xavier taught me I might have a heart, unfortunately."

"Unfortunately," Andrea echoed as her smile widened.

"Okay. To lay it out for you, I guess — if I don't have anything else going on that day — I'll be your maid of honor."

Andrea screeched and flung her arms around Chelsea. Chelsea cackled in spite of herself and burrowed her head into her friend's shoulder. Whoever was in charge of the music blared that old, silly song by Miley Cyrus — "Party in the USA," and everyone screamed out the lyrics. How old had Chelsea been when this song had come out? Gosh, it had been ten, eleven years before and she had been just an energetic, slightly wild eight-year-old. Probably, she'd sung the lyrics to her father in that old truck of his, and he had winced with the pain of it all.

What kind of songs would his new daughter sing for him? What would annoy him next?

"Guess what!" Andrea cried as she reached for Isaac's hand.

"What's up?" Isaac seemed half-pleased to be drawn away from Xavier's intense conversation.

"She said yes!"

Isaac grinned as his eyes met with Chelsea's. "To be honest, I don't think Andrea cares who she marries that day in December. She just wants you there as her maid of honor."

"Oh, stop. That's not totally true," Andrea said playfully as she winked at her fiancé.

"It kind of is. Trade me in for any one of these other dudes, as long as you get your Chelsea," Isaac teased, pulling her into his embrace and kissing the top of her head.

Xavier disappeared to grab them each another beer. Chelsea settled in closer against her friend and heaved an exhausted sigh. "So, Andi. What are you going to have me wear? Putrid green? Bright neon orange?"

"Oh my God, silly girl. I'll only have you wear neon salmon," Andrea returned, then burst out with laughter.

"Come on. What kind of horror are you going to create for me, Bridezilla?" Chelsea asked as she tried to poke her friend in the side but missed.

Their conversation sizzled on into the night. The party never went particularly off the rails, although, sometime after three in the morning, there was a very public breakup directly in front of them, beneath the gorgeous chandelier. The girl in the equation told the guy that she hated the drapes he had selected for the living room and that maybe, they should rethink this whole "moving in together" thing, anyway. The guy told the girl he hated everything she wore and the girl stormed off in clacking heels.

"I have to admit. Her outfit is atrocious," Andrea breathed into Chelsea's ear.

Chelsea cackled. "Don't talk too loudly. She might come back and stab you with one of those heels."

Later on, Chelsea and Andrea discussed various Vineyard

things — from the upcoming fundraiser to the events of the previous summer. It had been wild, especially on Andrea's end. Her father had somehow managed to lose an enormous amount of money to a fake investment firm, but they had gotten it all back, which had allowed Andrea to return to fashion school for this final semester.

"I was so worried I would just be working on that tour boat for the rest of my life," Andrea said as her eyes glowed with nostalgia. "Wearing that ridiculous outfit and talking to tourists non-stop about where to get the best ice cream cone on the island. I really could have killed my dad."

Chelsea swallowed the lump in her throat. "But you've found a way to forgive him?"

Andrea nodded. "Well, yes, of course. It's going to take a long time for me to get there. But I see how happy he's made Mom since he came back. And I know he's just as messed up as the rest of us. Now that I'm an adult, as scary as that sounds, I look at my parents for who they are. We're just trying to figure it all out as we go along. I have more compassion and empathy for them." She shrugged, then hurriedly added, "Not that you ever have to forgive your dad for what he did. He crossed a line that he'll never be able to cross back over, plus every circumstance is different."

Chelsea's eyes filled with tears, but she held them at bay. She wouldn't be just another girl crying at her first party in New York City.

"Naw. It doesn't matter," Chelsea said, even as her heart screamed with an intensity that yes, it truly did matter.

Later, as the night slowly blended and turned with the haze of the morning, Chelsea and Xavier walked and partly stumbled back to their tiny apartment. They paused at the doorway and kissed with longing, then immediately piled into bed and fell into a deep sleep. With her last conscious breaths, Chelsea's mind thanked her lucky stars for the first of hopefully many wild Brooklyn nights. She had craved this other life. And she still had Andrea and Xavier there, which represented pieces of home, as she launched herself forward into this new chapter.

CHAPTER SEVENTEEN

THE TOASTER HURLED two slices of toast into the air. Olivia touched the piping-hot slabs, dropped them onto plates, and turned to find Anthony, backpack over his shoulder and leather jacket on. She had insisted on feeding him before his trek off to Providence, where he would perform one of the greatest actions of his life: he would finalize his divorce, celebrate the end of an era with his daughter, crash at a hotel, then return to the island the following day. Olivia hustled up to him and pressed a kiss on his lips. She was overcome with longing to go with him but knew he had to do this alone. It was closure in his life; it had nothing to do with her.

"I can't believe I'll be single after today," Anthony said, teasing her.

"Yeah, you'll have to go out on the town. Pick up girls." Olivia wrapped her fingers around his neck and hung on him like a monkey to a tree. "Are you sure you have to go so soon?"

"I do." He flashed her that wicked grin, then said, "But I'll grab a piece of toast for the way."

Olivia knew full well that Anthony was the kind of man who could do anything himself. Tyler had been the sort to demand breakfast on the table; she'd found herself buttering and jamming his bread while he scrubbed up in the shower, already late for work. For this reason, however, Olivia relished caring for Anthony in this way. He half-protested when she scraped the butter across the toasted bread, then held up his hands and said, "You know you don't have to take care of me like that."

Olivia shrugged playfully. "I just don't trust you to do it correctly."

"So the truth comes out. She thinks I'm stupid, everyone."

Olivia rolled her eyes, placed the two pieces of toast on a paper towel, and then handed them over. "You'll drive safe?"

"No. I'll be all over the road at one hundred miles an hour."

"Be serious."

It was a Saturday morning. Olivia felt strange and outside of herself in the big house alone. She scrubbed the counters, cleaned out the fridge, and then checked on her various responsibilities for the upcoming fundraisers. She was waiting on four email responses, which meant she was at a standstill. She texted Amelia to explain the situation, and Amelia sent back a flurry of messages, highlighting the number of tasks she'd already managed to perform that morning, despite the fact that the day had only just begun.

OLIVIA: You're a monster, Amelia Taylor.

OLIVIA: Your baby is going to be a genius, isn't she?

OLIVIA: Ugh. Thank you for everything you're doing.

AMELIA: We'll get you that money, girl. I promise you that.

Olivia still wasn't so sure. She didn't want to lean too heavily on hope. She stood from her desk and stretched her arms over her head and considered what to do with her time. Papers, she supposed. They had piled up again. She'd asked students to choose their own adventure, as it were, when it came to topics. Thusly, she'd read a number of interesting ones, including "the significance of female characters in the novel," and "the metaphorical meaning of color," and "none of the characters in *The Great Gatsby* are happy, and here's why."

After about an hour of grading papers, Olivia began to read one titled, *"The Concept of Broken Hopes in The Great Gatsby."* Her heart began to patter wildly as she read her student's analyses of the various "hopes" the characters in *The Great Gatsby* had, many of which were defeated and how this represented a greater American dream and the subsequent loss of it.

"The thing about hopes is that we have to cling to them as long as we can, to give us some sort of drive, something to live for. Gatsby had Daisy; he always had Daisy. But it was just a facade. I wonder then, how many of our hopes are just that — empty vessels that we reach toward, thinking that once we retrieve them, all of our questions will be answered."

Olivia furrowed her brow and re-read the essay. It was remarkable and utterly moving, and it created a little black hole in the back of her mind. It demanded of her: what had she hoped for all these years? And did she have anything to reach for, now that The Hesson House had been wiped away?

It also demanded another question, one that had wormed around the back of her mind for several weeks. Did she really want to go on like this, year after year: eating bad lunches in the teacher's lounge, demanding kids read books they didn't want to read, and performing the same duties, year after year?

She had certainly loved teaching. Loved it! And for a long time, it had been enough. She had talked poetics about the beauty of filling teenagers' minds with literature, about activating their creative energies. All of that was still just as amazing as ever before. But she couldn't help but think, what was her story, exactly?

Would she really remain this empty shell, this endless giver of thought — without ever forming anything of her own?

Olivia finished grading the rest of the papers and placed the stack to the side. The late September early afternoon drew up a slight storm and splattered the glass with rain. Olivia's stomach jumped with fear as she hustled to her phone to check the weather. "Mild showers," it read. "Fifty-two degrees."

She heaved a sigh of relief. This wasn't hurricane weather. It was just a light drizzle.

Back in her study, Olivia sat in front of her computer and poised her fingers on the keyboard. A long, long time ago, before she had headed off to school to study teaching, she'd told her best friends that she wanted to be a writer. In the wake of that, she had thought if she couldn't be a writer, she could at least teach writing. That had been almost enough.

But maybe it wasn't enough any longer.

The act of writing was a bit like digging through all the

meaningless fluff and grabbing onto the creative side of things that one never knew existed. It's to push the boundaries of every word and description. It meant darting toward some sort of truth and drawing out fantastical things, beautiful images and thoughts and making them come alive on paper. Things in the dark recesses of her mind that she'd buried back there for years.

Eventually, she found herself writing poetics about her Great Aunt Marcia.

"She was an iconic woman: perpetually well-dressed, with this air of incredible intelligence, as though she already knew what you were about to say before you said it. Perhaps the love she had in her life was a more zealous and fiery sort of love — the type that burned out quickly and wasn't meant to last. I knew this better than most, as one afternoon after school, a handsome boy from school and I discovered her in the upstairs of an old mansion, pressed up against the wall by a younger man. She looked at me with these big, beautiful eyes — eyes that knew something and from that moment on, she felt we were linked. She attributed a level of courage to me that I don't believe I deserved. Perhaps, since that day, I've tried to build it within myself, against my nature. Perhaps Great Aunt Marcia would say that that's the only thing to do: fake your courage until you find it within yourself."

Olivia continued to write. She wrote about that young man her Great Aunt Marcia had had an affair with, whom she had later discovered was a relation to Anthony himself, which was part of the reason Anthony had been allowed to help build back up the old mansion in the first place. With each tap of her finger, each word scribed, Olivia felt closer and closer to some sort of identity she'd long since forgotten.

And goodness, with her love for her Great Aunt Marcia fluttering across the page like this, she missed her more than ever. She'd lost her aunt, and with the storm, she had lost The Hesson House. All she had left were her memories and she would ensure they would have a home, a place on the page. This was the only way.

Time seemed to speed up as Olivia wrote. She fell into a daze, one she was officially yanked from at around four o'clock when none other than Camilla Jenkins appeared in the window there in front of her desk. Apparently, she had jumped the fence in order to do just this: rap her knuckles on the glass and demand answers.

Olivia jumped from her desk and cried, "What the heck are you doing?"

Camilla's face brightened. She mouthed something — probably screaming it through the window, but Olivia couldn't make it out. She hustled out of the office and toward the back door, where she opened it to find the rest of the Sisters of Edgartown attempting to jump the fence to follow in Camilla's footsteps, save for Amelia, who stood off to the back instructing Jennifer on where to put her feet.

"What the heck are you doing? Are you all collectively robbing me? Because you should know, I don't have more than a few pennies to rub together."

"We've been calling you for hours!" Camilla said. "And then we knocked on your door and rang your doorbell the past ten minutes."

"Are you in some kind of fugue state?" Jennifer called.

"I was just—" Olivia hadn't thought she'd be caught in such a delicate act. She wasn't fully sure she wanted to share what she had been up to, even to her dearest friends. It was too precious. "I'm fine, but what about you? Is something wrong?"

"We want to go on an adventure," Mila announced mischievously.

"We decided we've all been working way too hard," Camilla affirmed. "Namely one of us." She glared at Amelia through the fence.

Amelia shook her head. "If I don't do it, it doesn't get done correctly."

"What kind of adventure?" Olivia asked.

Jennifer hobbled down the other side of the fence, giving up. "We have bottles of wine in the car and plenty of food."

"Say no more," Olivia said.

"And grab your coat. And extra blankets," Mila told her.

"Aye, aye, captain." Olivia rushed back inside, holding open the door so that Mila and Camilla could come in the back way and meet the others out front. As Olivia hunted through her closet for blankets, she said, "I can't believe you guys tried to break into my house."

"You didn't give us a choice, babe," Camilla said. "And it's what you girls did to me earlier this year, remember?"

Camilla had taken the separation from Jonathon incredibly hard. She'd boarded herself up in her bedroom, hardly showered, and avoided food. The Sisters of Edgartown had cleaned her up, organized her house, and helped her take each day at a time.

"We were worried about you, hon," Mila said as she took several of Olivia's blankets into her arms. "That's enough of a reason to break your door down, in my book."

Olivia returned briefly to her computer and saved all two

thousand words she had written that afternoon. For the first time in her adult life, she contemplated what it might be like to write a book — maybe a fictionalized account of the wonderfully wicked life of her Great Aunt Marcia. Perhaps she could even weave her own story within it, with a backdrop of The Hesson House. Perhaps in that small way, The Hesson House could live on, if they weren't able to build up the funds, that is.

CHAPTER EIGHTEEN

PERHAPS IT WASN'T ENTIRELY within the bounds of the law what they did next. They piled into Amelia's car — the five of them, despite there really being only space for four, and popped open the first bottle of champagne, which they passed between them in the back seat. Amelia clucked her tongue from the front seat and said, "If you girls get me into any trouble..."

"What? You're Amelia Taylor. Nobody can touch you on this island," Jennifer said brightly. She knocked her head back and took another gulp of champagne, which brought her elbow against Olivia's cheek.

"Hey!" Olivia cried.

In response, Jennifer dug her elbow even more into Olivia's cheek as Olivia dropped her head off to the left. Her laughter was raucous. "You're such a monster, Jennifer Conrad. The whole island thinks you're this good and kind and gracious woman, but we know the truth!"

Jennifer released the top of the bottle and cackled menacingly. She then passed the bottle off to Olivia, who leaned back and performed the same action. Champagne bubbles dotted across her tongue and danced down her throat as Amelia weaved her car down Captain's Walk and then westward, to who-knew-where. The Sisters of Edgartown had opted for an adventure and Olivia was along for the ride.

Camilla sat upfront. She gripped the champagne bottle when Mila passed it along, then met Olivia's gaze. "I forgot to talk to you about something!"

"What's up?" Olivia asked.

"Andrea finally asked Chelsea."

Olivia was surprised to hear her daughter's name. "Asked her what?" Her heart sped up the slightest bit; it was true that she and Chelsea had missed one another's phone calls the previous days. Their text messages were answered sparingly. It felt as though they drifted further and further apart, especially as Chelsea had made it so clear she didn't need her mother any longer.

"You know. To be her maid of honor for the wedding," Camilla affirmed.

"Oh, right. Well, that's wonderful news, isn't it?" Olivia wasn't sure her voice lent the amount of joy and light Camilla really wanted to hear. After all, her only daughter was getting married. It was probably one of the biggest events in Camilla's life.

"It really is! You remember when the girls were just little things, playing in the yard? And we joked that they'd be in one another's weddings some day, the way we were in each other's?" Camilla continued. "I can't believe it actually came true."

"Kind of rare these days, isn't it?" Mila interjected. "It seems like people are so volatile. They don't hold onto one another in the same way."

"Not our girls," Camilla said with a wink. She then turned to catch Mila's gaze and asked, "How is our girl, Isabelle, doing up at Tufts?"

Mila buzzed her lips. "Well, it was a tough road the first few weeks. She missed her boyfriend a lot."

Isabelle and her long-term boyfriend had broken up in the weeks leading up to their departure to their freshman years of college. Olivia could envision the heartache of all that — being eighteen and ready to take on the world, yet nursing an ache you couldn't fully name.

"But now, she's already told me she has her first college crush," Mila said. "In her poetry class."

"Uh oh. Poetry?" Amelia called from the front seat.

"That's right. What about it?" Mila asked.

"You don't want her to date some kind of heartbroken poet, do you?" Amelia said. "You know those artist types. They always think the world is out to get them."

Mila laughed. "I think Isabelle has to make her own mistakes when it comes to all that, unfortunately. And plus, Xavier is kind of like that, right, Olivia?"

Olivia wasn't sure what to say. She bit at her lower lip as the image of her greatest love, Chelsea, came to the forefront of her mind. What on earth were she and Xavier up to? Were they happy? Were they fed? Were they clean? She clutched her knees as her thoughts spiraled.

"Chelsea and Xavier both march to the beat of their own drum," Jennifer interjected when Olivia couldn't find the words.

"They sure do," Mila agreed. "And it's infectious. I think they were made for one another."

"I think they were, too," Olivia finally admitted somberly. "And what a wonderful thing it is to find true love."

AMELIA PARKED the car at the Aquinnah Cliffs Overlook. Jennifer drew open the back of the car and brought out two picnic baskets, one of which she passed over to Olivia. Olivia nearly dropped the thing.

"Ooph. What's in this?"

"Just a lot of wine," Jennifer said mischievously.

"And I guess you're carrying, what, bread and cheese?"

"Basically." Jennifer howled with laughter as she raced ahead of the others toward a little staircase that led from the top of the cliffs toward the beach below. Years before, they had traced this very path as teenagers, frequently bringing boys along with them. They'd split up into couples and kissed until the stars sprinkled in through the night sky above.

Now, as forty-one-year-olds, they took the steps a bit more delicately than they might have at seventeen. They swapped jokes about it — about how they'd have to put in a chairlift as the years went past, as they weren't about to give up their perfect spot, even into their eighties and nineties.

"I'll just get new knees implanted and I'll be right as rain," Mila joked.

"Gosh, I can't believe I'm going to be a mother at forty-two," Amelia said with a heavy sigh. She was up toward the back, with

Olivia right behind her to ensure that she wasn't left behind. "Imagine me! Forty-five, with a toddler?"

"We'll be right there with you," Olivia reminded her. "Going to pre-school graduations and cleaning up vomit."

"Hey. I didn't say I would do any of that vomit clean-up," Mila said from down below. "I did enough of that with the twins. I told Peter that at least we got all that icky stuff out of the way in one go."

"Well, I'll be there for you, in any case," Olivia said with a laugh.

When they reached the beach below, they gathered on blankets and then wrapped themselves up in still thicker blankets so that they created a kind of ecosystem of warmth, even as the wind threatened to rip through them. The waves frothed against the rocks and barreled against the cliffs in the distance. Jennifer removed several different types of cheeses from the picnic basket and positioned them out across the blankets, and then brought out freshly-baked bread, which she said came from Christine Sheridan.

"How is the rebuild for the Sunrise Cove Bistro going?" Olivia asked.

"Actually, the kitchen itself wasn't damaged at all, so they're doing okay with baked goods," Jennifer said. "Christine is pretty dang pregnant. I have to say — maybe a month or so ahead of you, Amelia? But she says she likes to stay busy. It keeps her mind off things. Oh, and I spotted Baby Max through the window. Zach Walters carried him around on his shoulder. He looked like a proud dad."

"He better. He took off after the baby was born," Mila said pointedly.

"True. But he came back," Camilla pointed out. "After what

happened between Jonathon and me, I have to make space for forgiveness for other people. We're all just trying to figure everything out."

They held the silence for a moment. Mila poured them each bubbly glasses of champagne, while Amelia took out a bottle of sparkling water and poured it into a champagne glass. They clinked glasses and then cheered the ocean, that monstrous and untamable beast — the source of so much pleasure and so much insurmountable pain. For a long moment, Olivia could sense each of them thinking about Michelle, about how they missed her and wished she had been allowed all the decades of life they'd lived.

Even Chelsea, now, was older than Michelle had been when she'd died. Isabelle, Andrea and Mandy all were, too. Olivia could only thank the stars above that they'd made it through their childhoods. They were allowed to make adult decisions. They were allowed to figure out who they wanted to become.

"Come on, Olivia. We lost you again." This was Jennifer, whose eyes latched onto Olivia's.

"What? Oh. I'm sorry."

"I feel like you're in your own world lately," Mila replied. She lifted a strand of hair around Olivia's ear and dropped her chin. "We just want you to know that — well — we can't possibly understand what it means to you to lose The Hesson House right now."

"You put your heart and soul into that place all year long," Camilla said.

"Come on, girls. It's not a person. It's just a house," Olivia said doubtfully.

"But it represented a new era for you," Amelia pointed out softly.

Olivia's eyes watered with the wind. She dropped her chin toward her chest and felt the first of many tears drop. "I felt kind of on top of the world during those first few weeks," she admitted finally. "Frantic, yes, but also, I felt like if I could just get through that first year, me and Anthony would be golden. We would have everything we ever dreamed for."

"It was such a beautiful space," Mila breathed. "I don't think I loved a place more on the Vineyard."

"At least there are photos," Olivia said with a funny shrug. "I can look back at this small era of my life and say, hey, I did something different. For once, I wasn't too afraid to make a change."

Their conversations continued on as sunlight dimmed over the horizon just there, off to the west, cascading into oranges and pinks, which billowed out across the waves. Another bottle of wine was uncorked, and eventually, after another few glasses were drunk, Mila dared Jennifer to take off everything but her bra and underwear and run into the waves.

"It's freezing!" Jennifer cried.

"Come on. You would have done it if you were eighteen," Mila pointed out.

"But I'm not eighteen," Jennifer returned.

Mila leaped up and hurriedly removed her jacket and sweater. She stood — a sturdy, slender woman, in just her bra, then crossed her arms over her chest and gave Jennifer a pointed look.

"Come on, Jen. If you don't swim with me in the Nantucket Sound right this minute, then I swear I don't know who you are anymore."

Jennifer rolled her eyes as the other Sisters of Edgartown hooted and hollered. As Mila and Jennifer raced off in just their underwear and bra, Olivia and Camilla and Amelia chased after them. Camilla and Olivia flung their clothes out behind them then thrust their legs through the air until their feet rushed up against the first onslaught of the chilly waves. Olivia's screams joined the others. Their voices were a cacophony; their screams bounced off the cliff sides and then headed into the night sky above.

Not so long after, the four dripping-wet and freezing girls wrapped up in blankets grabbed their things and hustled back to the car, making sure not to go too quickly, as Amelia had a belly to take up with her. Back up at the top, they demanded that Amelia turn up the heat as high as it would go — and also stop at the Edgartown pizza place for three large pizzas.

"We didn't get through much of the cheese, and I'm starving," Camilla said.

"I can agree with you four delinquents on that," Amelia said as she crept the heat higher and higher. "I can't believe you got in the Sound. It's almost October, you know!"

"See, Amelia? You already sound like a mom," Olivia said with a laugh. "You'll be a natural."

CHAPTER NINETEEN

THEY WERE OUT OF SILVERWARE. It was the height of the night — eight-fifteen, with countless four-tops and two-tops, families and dates looking to take in some of Manhattan's finest cuisine, pouring in from the streets, their eyes bright and their moods easily shifted from intrigue and excitement toward annoyance at the wait-time. Chelsea scrambled through the just-washed silverware, stabbed it into linen napkins, and rolled up as though her life depended on it. Within the kitchen, on the other side of the open window between where the servers picked up their plates and the kitchen staff created their masterpieces, Marty howled at Chelsea. "Hurry up out there. We have hungry guests, and they're getting angry."

"You think I don't know that? I just got stiffed. Ten percent tip? Don't they know what the economy is like?" Chelsea barreled back.

She shot back into the nightmare of the dining area, where she prepped a table evenly, just as one of the hostesses guided a family of four toward that very table. Chelsea brightened her face into a false smile.

"Good evening, everyone," she said as she presented drink menus to the father, the mother, and their two twenty-something daughters — neither of whom seemed particularly pleased to be there.

"Evening," the father spouted. "I'd like a Negroni, as soon as you can make it."

"Dad, you don't have to get wasted the minute we go out together," one of the girls pointed out.

"Alyssa!" the woman cried.

"What are you doing? You're not my mother," the girl named Alyssa returned.

"Alyssa. Maggie. I asked to have a pleasant evening out tonight," their father said, his words firm. "You've known Maxine your entire lives. The least you can do is show her a modicum of respect."

Maggie and Alyssa exchanged disgruntled glances. Chelsea felt a story brewing beneath the surface of this one, but she didn't have enough time to dig in deep.

"Negroni. And what can I get the rest of you?"

The man arched a thick eyebrow and then asked that horrendous question — something Chelsea resented eternally, no matter if she worked at Tiny Tim's or at the diner back home. "Aren't you going to write down our order? I hate when waitresses don't write down the order. They inevitably get it wrong."

"Dad. This woman is clearly a professional," Maggie blurted.

Annoyed, Chelsea grabbed her notepad and faked writing out "Negroni" in blue pen. The woman, apparently named Maxine, ordered a glass of Prosecco, while the two daughters both ordered Pinot Grigio. Chelsea told them the evening's menu, something that was ever-changing. Immediately after, Alyssa pointed out that Chelsea didn't seem to have a difficult time remembering that "rather extensive" menu. Her father looked past her as though she didn't exist.

"Happy family," Chelsea muttered to herself as she fled the table like it was the scene of a crime.

Chelsea had seven tables at this moment — seven tables of very hungry and very loud New Yorkers. Her previous lovely notions regarding New Yorkers had fled, at least for the night, and lent her this sinister feeling about all people, no matter what. They were all hungry and greedy and volatile, and they looked at her as though she was the devil incarnate.

Just after she had ordered up the non-family of four's menu items, one of the kitchen staff members hollered through the window to tell her that she had a phone call in the office.

"What? That's impossible." Chelsea balked at him.

"Nope. You have a call. And they said it's urgent."

"Nothing is as urgent as what I have going on out here," Chelsea told him. "I'm putting out almost literal fires out here."

This wasn't true, of course, but it certainly felt like it. Her anxiety skyrocketed.

"Should we tell the guy who says it's an emergency that you don't care about him?" another of the kitchen staff members piped up.

"I don't see why you would do that." Chelsea's nostrils flared with annoyance. She scrubbed her hands on her apron and then rushed in through the swiveling kitchen door. Once in the steam of the kitchen, she rushed toward the back door of the office, then grabbed the phone and placed it on her ear. It had been ages since she'd used an actual landline.

"This is Chelsea speaking."

For a long moment, there was silence. Of course. The kitchen staff had decided to play a cruel joke on her. They had seen how slammed she'd been; they wanted to yank her out of her groove and make her even later with her next course. The time she spent within these four office walls literally ate her tips away.

"Listen, if there's actually somebody there, you're wasting my time. I have about a zillion things to do, and the fact that you've just called me out of the blue during my shift is absolutely inconsiderate and borderline evil, to be honest with you."

She spat the words with vitriol.

And a moment later, a very familiar voice answered.

"Chelsea, I'm sorry. I'm really so sorry."

It was her father. She hadn't spoken to him at all since she'd left the city. She'd only heard from him once — when she had texted him to ask if he was all right. Now, here he was.

"Dad."

Tears sprung to her eyes. Back in her teenage years, having her father call had felt like Christmas Day. She'd found all sorts of things to tell him to keep him on the phone longer. She would even make up stories just to make herself sound more interesting, more intelligent.

"I know you're busy. I know that place can fill up like nobody's business," Tyler continued.

Chelsea's throat tightened. In the doorway, Marty stood. He mouthed at her, "What the hell are you doing?" But she turned her back to him and lifted a finger to tell him she just needed a minute.

"I need to talk to you," Tyler said finally. "In person."

Chelsea had no idea what to say. She was paralyzed.

"I'll come to the city on your next day off," he continued. "Just tell me where to meet you, and I'll be there."

Chelsea felt like she was in a nightmare. Every muscle in her body screamed for her to say no, that she couldn't hack it. She couldn't manage to be his daughter if he planned to yank her around like this.

"I'm off tomorrow," Chelsea said finally. Immediately, she cursed herself. How could she just give him all of herself like this? How could she be so weak?

"I'll be there bright and early. With bagels and coffee," her father said.

"Okay. Meet me at my place; I guess," Chelsea told him. "You know where it is."

"I do." He sighed. "See you."

Chelsea pressed past Marty without making eye contact. He demanded to know just what she thought she was doing, talking on the phone when her tables awaited their food, their drinks, their bills, and their change. She threw her hands through the air and yearned to quit but held back the words. She couldn't just run from this like she had before with her father and Xavier.

Again, Chelsea appeared over the table of the man and his daughters, along with the woman they seemed not to care for, named Maxine. The daughters had hardly touched their meals. They blinked at Maxine as though she was a horrible specimen to be studied in a lab. Chelsea noticed now that one of the girls wore a wedding ring; she wondered where the husband was.

There was such awkwardness at the table. Tense air stretched over the four of them. When Chelsea asked, "How is everything so far?" they hardly blinked at her.

But after a moment, the father turned his eyes toward her and asked, "We're absolutely fine, thank you. And you? You're not from the city, are you? Where are you from?"

Chelsea got this sometimes: customers who pretended to be interested in her backstory, if only because they were bored or annoyed with their company.

"Oh, I'm from Martha's Vineyard," Chelsea returned.

Normally, this news was received warmly. Often, people said, "Oh, we've vacationed there," or, "Oh, our friends were married there."

But this time, the mood at the table erupted like lightning. The daughters' smiles were enormous; Maxine's face fell toward the ground, and the father, well, all the color drained from his cheeks.

"I'm sorry. Did I say something wrong?" Chelsea now had the feeling that she'd stirred the pot even more.

"Our mother lives there," Alyssa piped up, clearly excited. "And Maggie just got married there a few weeks ago."

"Oh! That's exciting," Chelsea replied, flashing them all a huge smile.

"Yeah. It was a beautiful wedding," their father said in an icy tone.

"It was supposed to be," Maggie returned.

"Come on. I told you how much I spent on that wedding of yours," her father said, bristling.

Maggie threw her hands skyward. Chelsea's eyes connected with Alyssa's as she asked, "Where does your mother live?"

"Oh, she works for Katama Lodge and Wellness Spa," she said. "Our grandmother and step-aunts work there, too. We spent a lot of time there over the summer. It's such a beautiful place!"

"Wow. Were you there for the hurricane?"

"No, thank goodness," Alyssa returned. "I would have totally freaked."

"I was on my honeymoon," Maggie told her.

"One of three," her father affirmed.

"Dad!" Maggie blurted.

Chelsea's smile widened. "Well, just let me know if you four need anything else. Another negroni, perhaps?"

"Absolutely. And keep them coming," the father returned.

Chelsea sauntered back to the computer, where she pressed in their new drink orders, humming to herself. One of the bartenders asked her, "What are you so happy about?" And Chelsea wasn't fully sure she knew the answer.

"I guess it's just good to know that other people have messed up families," she said as she pressed the "SEND" button on the computer.

"Yeah? Does that surprise you?" the bartender asked.

"Naw," Chelsea replied. "Just gives me strength that I can handle my own stuff."

"You go get 'em, Chels," the bartender said. "I have absolutely no idea what you're talking about, but I believe in you, girl. But right now, I'm going to need you to go greet that new table. They look like chickens with their heads cut off. Where's the hostess?"

Chelsea sped through the dining room, smiling warmly at the

new guests. "Welcome to Tiny Tim's," she said, feeling like a top-grade waitress, the kind who deserved upwards of a thirty-percent tip. "Let me show you to your table."

CHAPTER TWENTY

XAVIER FILLED a mug of coffee and placed it on the counter between the two of them. His eyes glistened as he struggled to hold in the thoughts Chelsea could practically see scurrying around in his mind. He wasn't sure he supported Chelsea's decision to see her father after the mess he'd made. But Chelsea had said, point-blank, that this was what she wanted to do. "I can handle myself," she told him again, just before she took an overly large sip of piping hot coffee and then had to spit it into the sink.

"Yeah. You really look like you can handle yourself," Xavier said playfully. He grabbed a paper towel and passed it over as Chelsea stewed in embarrassment. His hand glided across her shoulder and down her waist as he added, "I'm just worried. He's a poisonous person. I don't want him to trap you again."

"He won't," Chelsea said. "Maybe I'm a stupid optimist for saying that, but. I won't let him come into our house again. It'll all be out in the open. Whatever fight we get into. Whatever mess we make. It won't be here. And it won't affect you."

Chelsea dressed in the bedroom while Xavier flicked through YouTube videos in the living room. First, she opted for jeans and a dark yellow sweater; then, she discarded those, tugged on tights and a skirt and a black sweater, and then fingered her hair to give it more volume. Makeup was essential, but how much of it was appropriate? She wanted to look powerful, regal, a bit older than her nineteen years, but she also didn't want Tyler to think she had run so far away from her youthful past. Parents were tricky; Tyler was an advanced version of that.

"You look good," Xavier told her as she stepped back into the living room.

Chelsea shrugged and collected her keys. It was five minutes to eleven, their set meeting time. She half-expected him to be tardy. Like some kind of fool, she hovered near the window and watched the street outside. They were two floors up, which allowed her unique perspective on the passers-by. When a man in a trench coat hovered near the corner, as though he considered turning back, she made her way for the door and hollered, "I'll see you later, Xav. Love you!" She then rushed down the staircase and burst into the chilly October morning.

Her father remained at the corner. He held a bag of bagels, just as he'd promised, along with two coffee cups in a little cardboard container. His eyes found Chelsea's, and he gave her a foolish smile. She had caught him in the midst of a fearful tirade. She wouldn't let him run back to Boston without a conversation. At nineteen, she would no longer accept her father's fear.

"Hi." She greeted him without a smile.

He passed her the coffee and nodded. Since she'd last seen him, he'd gained a bit of healthy weight. His cheeks had filled out and now glowed a peachy pink. In a moment, Chelsea knew.

"Casey had the baby."

Her father nodded and then repeated the words as though they held such meaning that it was difficult to take it in.

"Casey had the baby."

Chelsea's shoulders fell forward. She led her father toward a little bench across the street, where she dropped her head the slightest bit and considered this enormous fact: somewhere in Boston, she had a baby sister. Her father was a new father again.

Tyler sat a few inches from Chelsea on the bench, conscious that she needed the space. He bowed his head and snaked his fingers together.

"Her name is Ava," he said finally.

"That's a beautiful name."

"She's beautiful," Tyler affirmed. "It suits her."

Chelsea sniffled. Why was she crying? She felt so silly. She sipped her coffee and then asked to see a photo of the baby. Obviously, Tyler's phone was already filled with them. There little Ava was: sleeping against Casey's chest, just a few minutes after coming into the world. There she was, yawning the most adorable yawn as her eyes took in a fresh world. There she was, over and over again, in a million little positions that were very nearly the same as the ones before.

There was so much to say. Chelsea's throat tightened. Should she just throw out her own emotions, replace them with joy for her baby sister? But wasn't that the cowardly thing to do — not to face that which had tied you all up inside?

"What happened to you? After you left the city?" Chelsea finally asked as Tyler slipped his phone back into his pocket.

Tyler buzzed his lips. "I tried again to contact Casey. I knew the due date wasn't long off. Still, she wouldn't talk to me, so I checked into rehab. Insane, isn't it? I just felt I couldn't handle anything anymore."

"Wow." Chelsea had never had a more adult conversation in her life, maybe. She felt shaky.

"I was there for seven days. It was really all we could afford but worth every penny," Tyler told her. "And I managed to reach out to Casey from there. She came to visit me. I've never seen anyone angrier with me. Not even your mom. Never make a pregnant woman mad. But she hugged me, she cried and she told me that she still loved me and wanted me in the baby's life. I just have to be there and show up in every way. And I have to stop drinking. So, after I got back home, I joined AA. More than that, I even got a therapist."

"Self-improvement is a huge time suck," Chelsea said with a slight laugh.

"Tell me about it. I feel like I'm constantly trying to better myself these days. It's exhausting. Do you want to know what I had for breakfast before I left this morning? A smoothie. I don't even recognize myself anymore."

Chelsea chuckled as a wave of warmth came over her. Again, she sipped her coffee. What did anyone say to such a story? How could she possibly translate how much it meant to her?

"I'm so proud of you," she whispered. "Really."

Tyler nodded. His eyes seemed very far away. "It's going to be a really long road."

"Yes. But you're already much further than you were."

"They do say to take it one day at a time," Tyler said. "I'm already spouting AA logic."

"AA logic works for thousands of people," Chelsea said. "I don't see any reason why it wouldn't work for you."

They walked for a while, in no particular direction, without any kind of assessment of the time. Eventually, they ordered another cup of coffee each and sat at a different bench, where they dug into the bagels like they hadn't eaten all day.

"This is not a smoothie," Tyler said between bites. "It's magic."

Two pigeons hobbled around in front of them on the sidewalk; one of them had lost a leg, but he didn't seem to notice it. He hopped around with his head held high.

"I miss the birds on the Vineyard sometimes," Tyler said softly. "In the cities, it's just pigeons everywhere. I remember the wide selection we would get in the backyard at our place. Your mom set up that bird feeder, and she would whisper to me when a particularly beautiful one would come up to eat."

Chelsea laughed, even as pain latched around her heart and threatened to take her down.

"The bird feeder is still there," Chelsea told him. "And the birds still come."

"Incredible," Tyler replied. He then dropped his bagel the slightest bit as he said, "I read more about The Hesson House. I actually thought about reaching out to your mom. I don't know. She probably has enough on her plate without worrying about me."

"But she does worry about you. Why wouldn't she?" Chelsea returned.

Tyler nodded. After another pause, he said, "I was never very kind to your mom. I guess you know that."

Chelsea couldn't breathe. This was the heinous truth. This was what she'd always longed to look away from.

"I think I was a frightened little kid. And then I turned into a frightened man. And I thought that marrying Olivia was the right thing to do."

"Didn't you ever love her? At all?"

Tyler considered this. "Of course, I did. In my own way, I loved her. But we were so different. I could see it in everyone's eyes at the wedding. Nobody understood why we were getting married. Even my groomsmen asked me before the ceremony if I wanted to duck out."

"Jesus."

"I'm sorry to tell you that."

"No. It's okay. I wanted honesty and here it is. Honesty." Chelsea's stomach flipped over. She chewed at the same small morsel of bagel-and-cream-cheese a little too much, then swallowed. Finally, she forced herself to say something she had never imagined telling her father.

"You really hurt me, Dad. When you left."

Tyler's head dropped again. "I know."

"No. I don't know if you really do. I felt like I'd done something wrong. I waited for you to come back. I blamed Mom for everything. I turned into this monster teenager. And then, the minute I leave the island, you come parading into my new life as though you've been waiting for me the entire time. I don't know when I'll get over that or if I ever will."

Tyler's eyes glistened. Chelsea prayed he wouldn't cry.

"I can't even begin to make any of that up to you," Tyler finally said. "The only thing I can extend now is an invitation into my new life. I know that's not fair. And Chelsea, I'm so sorry for all of it. I know there aren't enough words in the dictionary to describe how I feel about any of it. Just that I am so sorry. And I am fighting, every single day, to be the kind of person you deserve in your life."

Chelsea squeezed her eyes shut. The emotion felt similar to a tidal wave.

Finally, she forced herself to speak. The silence between them was too powerful; she could drown in it.

"I want to meet her," she whispered. "I want to know Ava. I want to be in her life and in yours."

Tyler wrapped an arm around Chelsea's shoulder and tugged her into him. Her chin quivered with sorrow. Already, she could see the future before them — her holding baby Ava as her father took a clumsy photo; Casey doting on the little presents Chelsea brought in from New York City; little Ava gazing up at her with impossible wonder as Chelsea promised to care for her.

She would. She would be the kind of big sister this little creature needed. She would be there for her in everything.

"You know," Tyler finally said as they wandered back toward Chelsea's corner of Brooklyn. "When you went back to the Vineyard and I was left with that boyfriend of yours, I really took a liking to him."

Chelsea laughed with surprise. "Did you?"

"Yes. He's such a good guy," Tyler affirmed. "I mean, he probably hates me more than I can ever recover from. But I trust him. I trust him with you and that makes me happy."

The Autumn sun was a different breed of sun. It was gentle

and forgiving and further away, as though already thinking about the horror it had committed over the summer months. An eggshell blue sky stretched over them; not a single cloud flickered through to ruin it. It was as though the day had been drawn with a child's crayon.

"I love you, Dad," Chelsea murmured when they paused at the door. She hugged him and then added, "Don't drink too many smoothies. You'll get your cool card revoked."

"I always knew I'd have to give that thing up one of these days," Tyler said as he stepped back. "See you soon, I hope, Chels. Casey, Ava and I will be waiting."

CHAPTER TWENTY-ONE

THE HURRICANE RELIEF fundraiser was held on the second Saturday of October at the Harbor View Hotel. Some said the hotel had graciously donated their space; others said that Amelia Taylor had twisted someone's arm in upper management. Regardless of which story was true, set-up for the hurricane fundraiser began at eight-thirty in the morning and brought in nearly fifty people, including the Sisters of Edgartown, their romantic partners, and any children who happened to be around. Staff members from the Harbor View hustled about, instructing islanders on where extra tables were stored, where to set up the various stalls, and how they should construct the auction area, which was the space that would assuredly bring in the most revenue. Comfort was of utmost importance.

Olivia and Chelsea carried a long table out from the side entrance of the hotel. Olivia was impressed with Chelsea's strength and embarrassed with her own lack of it. "Can we just pause for one sec?" Olivia cried, gasping. "I don't know where you got those biceps. Not from my side of the family."

Chelsea's laughter was bright. "You should see some of the trays I have to carry at the restaurant. Plates piled on top of plates with a million little glasses of wine portioned out across, perfectly balanced."

"You're flirting with disaster, Chelsea girl," Olivia said.

"Naw. I'm just a professional."

Anthony and Oliver, Amelia's boyfriend, whipped past in conversation about how precisely to set up the chairs for the auction area. Toward the far end of the grounds, Camilla and Jennifer set up another of the games, one of the ones that involved fake guns and little targets. They'd reused a number of games from various Edgartown and Oak Bluffs festivals over the years. Beyond them, near the beach, Amelia held court over a selection of Harbor View employees, presumably about how to set up the rest of the space. According to their plans, a bonfire would be held near the beach, along with a number of wine and food kiosks. Amelia had a very elaborate map and, according to her, a near-perfect strategy.

"You think this will actually work?" Olivia asked Chelsea as they continued to amble with the table toward the finish line.

"Yes. I have to believe it will," Chelsea told her.

"Where did all that optimism come from?" Olivia asked. "I know they don't sell it in the city."

Chelsea chuckled but refused to answer. Olivia was just grateful she'd decided to come to the island for the fundraiser. They had hardly spoken in recent weeks; then, out of the blue, Chelsea had texted that she and Xavier planned to return for two days.

"Can we stay with you?" she'd asked, as Xavier wasn't too keen on seeing his family again.

Naturally, Olivia had opened her house, her arms, and her heart. She would always be there for Chelsea, no matter what. It was what being a mother meant.

The set-up work was grueling and took several hours. Around ten-thirty, Amelia finally set up a speaker system to make things lighter and more interesting. Sandwiches were called in from the hotel restaurant, and the set-up workers sat around, sweating from the labor, yet chilly with the October breeze. Amelia waddled around slowly and bossed everyone around, as was her way, even as Oliver hopped after her, asking if she might want to sit down soon. She just glared at him.

"Amelia's on the warpath," Jennifer whispered as she sat alongside Chelsea and Olivia. "I saw her almost bite Camilla's head off earlier."

Olivia chuckled. "That's our girl. An absolute maniac."

"There's Xavier! And Andrea!" Chelsea stood and waved the two over. Andrea's blonde luscious hair caught the sunlight beautifully. She rushed toward Chelsea, wrapped her arms around her waist, and then lifted her into the air with a screech.

"I didn't think you were coming!" Chelsea cried.

"I didn't think so, either," Andrea admitted. "And then I thought about it for about five minutes more and realized I had to come. The island needs me." She blushed and then added, "That sounds ridiculous, doesn't it?"

"No. It sounds like you're a superhero," Chelsea teased. "The island needs me!" She shot a hand into the air, mocking superman, as Andrea cackled.

Olivia's heart grew at the sight of this. She loved watching this next generation of best friends — the direct lineage of the Sisters of Edgartown — laugh and joke like this. It meant that the Sisters of Edgartown were so much more than just the five-some; their love had extended out. It would last forever, even as they passed on from this earth.

Jennifer felt it, too. She gripped Olivia's hand and whispered, "I curse every day that I only had a boy. You're so lucky!"

Olivia laughed. "You weren't complaining as much as we were when he was a teenager, though. Nick was a dream compared to Chelsea and Andrea."

"True," Jennifer said thoughtfully. "I can't believe he'll be married soon and Andrea, too. And jeez, Chelsea's headed in that direction, as well."

"I know. Adults, doing adult things. How dare they?" Olivia teased.

"Somebody has to put a stop to it. And I hope it's Amelia because I don't know if I have the strength for it," Jennifer said.

The set-up continued until two. The fundraiser itself was set to begin at three-thirty, which left the set-up crew an hour or so to relax, kick back, and contemplate the hours ahead. According to Amelia's polls, most of the island was slated to come out to the fundraiser and there was plenty for them to throw their money at.

"I also have some high-rollers coming in from the city," Amelia informed them thoughtfully as she checked out her clipboard, which seemed the source of all human knowledge. "So I'm hoping they buy some of the bigger ticket items at the auction."

"Thank you, Amelia. You've really nailed this," Olivia praised her as she gazed out across the sea of game booths, food kiosks, little bars and the big stage near the beach and bonfire, where they would have a selection of local bands performing throughout the afternoon and evening.

"I could have done it in my sleep," Amelia lied with a smile. "The last thing we have to do is assign who mans which table. Xavier? Chelsea? I thought you could head up the Gone Fishing game?" It was a rhetorical question, although everyone knew what Amelia said was gold — unquestioned.

"Fine with us," Chelsea said as she and Xavier shared a playful high-five.

"Olivia? You and Anthony are at the bobbing for apple booth," Amelia instructed.

"Messy," Olivia said.

"Gross," Anthony affirmed.

The other games were passed out to others. Jennifer and Derek headed up the "Fortune Teller" game, which meant that they were about to make up a whole lot of futures for a whole lot of drunken islanders. Jennifer rubbed her palms together excitedly as Derek grumbled. "This is nothing I ever had to do back in the city," he said. "I know. And aren't you glad you moved to the island for all this wholesome fun?" Jennifer returned.

Andrea and her fiancé, Isaac, walked toward the far end of the fair to head up one of the bars while Camilla and Jonathon decided to monitor the baby animal tent.

"We have a baby animal tent?" Olivia asked.

"We have everything," Amelia affirmed. "Don't question it."

Olivia whistled as her fingers laced through Anthony's. "The woman has lost her mind."

"She's going to raise The Hesson House that million. You just watch and see," Anthony said. "And she's going to do it the only way she knows how. Intensely."

"Intensely. Yes. Exactly." Olivia's laughter swelled over them as they circled out toward their carnival game, where they would spend the next few hours or at least until their selection of apples ran dry.

CHAPTER TWENTY-TWO

PEOPLE ARRIVED at the fundraiser in droves. It was difficult to imagine that there were people anywhere else on the island; they seemed completely concentrated there on the Harbor View grounds. Everywhere, people munched on cotton candy and hustled from game to game. Children latched onto their father's hands and dragged them wildly toward their next prospect; prizes were passed into their tiny hands as their eyes glowed with wonder. Music swirled out from the concert area as Zach Walters' local band worked through their classic tracks — songs that everyone on the island knew by then, along with several radio hits from years past. As yet another apple-dunker appeared before their festival game, Anthony whispered, "I can't imagine this night not becoming an absolute success."

It was a hilarious thing, heading up the apple-dunker tent. It seemed similar to torture. One of the first couples who arrived was Nick and his fiancé, Stacy. Stacy ate caramel corn as she instructed

Nick to bob in and grab an apple with his perfect, bright white teeth. Nick eyed Olivia doubtfully.

"I don't know if I can do it. Is it rigged?"

"It's not rigged. But it's not the easiest game, either," Olivia told him.

Nick puffed out his cheeks. "I can't believe you're making me do this," he told Stacy.

"It's for the good of the island that you embarrass yourself in front of me like this," Stacy told him.

"Are you going to take a photo?"

"Absolutely. Our future children need to see this."

Nick rolled his eyes. "Here goes nothing."

"Three tickets, please," Olivia instructed.

Stacy passed over the tickets as Nick assembled himself before the large bucket of bulbous apples. He inhaled deeply so that his belly bulged out over his jeans. He then dunked himself forward, teeth-first, and remarkably, latched onto an apple, his very first try. Olivia and Anthony howled as Stacy flashed a perfect photograph. Nick turned and tapped Stacy on the head with the apple. It fell from his teeth as he rollicked with laughter.

"I told you I could do it, babe," he beamed. "Never doubt me again."

"I never will," Stacy replied with a laugh.

Nick selected a tiny teddy bear, which he presented to Stacy with child-like glee. They padded away, headed for the drink tent as Olivia and Anthony added a few more apples to the bucket. Nick had been the first to actually successfully grab an apple; the others had flailed around horribly before giving up, defeated.

"Do you think you could do it?" Olivia asked.

"If you think I'm about to embarrass myself in front of you like that, then you have another thing coming," Anthony told her.

"Come on," Olivia said, squeezing his hand and bouncing it around playfully.

Anthony sighed, took a swig of beer, and then dropped to his knees. "Okay. But only for you." He poised himself over the apples, eyeing them from multiple angles. He then flung himself forward, teeth-first, the way Nick had — but immediately came up gasping for breath, apple-less. Olivia's laughter rang out and she dropped down to try to lift him up.

"Okay! I get it. You're not good at this," she said.

Anthony blinked several times. Water dribbled from his eyelashes. He gestured for her to stand again, and then said he planned to try one more time. Olivia did as she was told. Several onlookers gathered, including Camilla and Jonathon, who'd traded out their stance at their table to make the rounds.

"Okay, Olivia. On the count of three," Anthony blurted out with a playful grin. "One - two - three."

But this time, Anthony didn't dunk down to grab an apple. Instead, he lifted something out of his pocket — a tiny black box and turned toward her to open it, even as he remained on his knees.

There, in the tiny black box, glinted a perfect princess cut diamond ring. Olivia's eyes found Anthony's. Shock permeated through her body.

"Olivia. Will you make me the happiest man on earth? Will you marry me?"

Olivia gasped and covered her mouth with a hand. The crowd around them hollered with glee at the surprise proposal. Suddenly, Olivia placed her hands over his wrists to try and tug him up into her; she wanted his arms around her as she shook with the joyful ecstasy of this moment. For a long time, she allowed silence to stretch between them. And when her eyes filled with tears, she finally whispered, "Yes. I will marry you. Of course, I'll marry you."

Anthony leaped to his feet. The crowd roared around them as he kissed her, bending her over backward like some kind of movie star. In the distance, Chelsea's voice rang out as she hollered, "MOM! Mom?" Olivia broke her perfect kiss to find her daughter weaving her way through the onlookers. She stopped on the other side of the apple bucket, sporting a tearful expression of her own.

"You did it?" she cried. "You finally did it?"

Olivia realized, then, that Chelsea had known all along. Probably, that was part of the reason she had come home in the first place.

"I finally did it. I didn't chicken out," Anthony told her. His hand found the small of Olivia's back as Chelsea leaped over the apple bucket and flung her arms around Olivia. Olivia felt suddenly very, very small, as her daughter held onto her as though the world spun wildly around them and she was apt to fly away.

When Chelsea leaned back, she made heavy eye contact with her mother as she said, "You deserve all the happiness in the world. I know you didn't have it for a long, long time."

Olivia was taken aback by the honesty of Chelsea's words. But before she could answer, Jennifer, Camilla, Amelia, and Mila all found their way to the apple-dunk game, where more hugs and kisses and congratulations were passed around. With every dramatic beat of her heart, Olivia was reminded again: she was engaged to marry the love of her life. In every sense of the word, the fundraiser was a success.

She had found the man of her dreams. And in their marriage, they would form a united front, a family of two — plus Chelsea and his daughter back in Providence. Their memories and the people they'd once been would be along for the ride as they continued to craft who they were and who they planned to be together.

AROUND EIGHT THAT EVENING, Anthony and Olivia stood just outside the auction area and watched the show of it all. Antique wardrobes, expensive lamps from sixty years ago, old handmade tables, furniture from the forties — each item was brought in, described by the professional auctioneer, then auctioned off to the various high-spenders in the audience, who lifted their numbers as the cost grew higher and higher.

"Remember, folks. This is all for a good cause," the auctioneer said, just before the cost of a particularly beautiful armoire jumped up to ten thousand dollars.

"He really knows how to work it," Anthony whispered, impressed.

Amelia ambled past them, her brow furrowed. Olivia caught her attention, despite Amelia's best efforts to avoid her. Amelia plastered a fake smile on her face and congratulated them again on the engagement. But Olivia knew there was something sinister beyond that expression.

"What's up?" Olivia demanded.

Amelia heaved a sigh. "It's just that we're not quite at our goal.

We've raised quite a bit of money—no doubt about that. But if we're going to portion everything out to other hotels and businesses across the island, we're not even close to the amount we need for The Hesson House. I hate to say that, but it's the truth."

Olivia's heart grew shadowed. "It's okay," she lamented softly. "It was a really good try."

Amelia buzzed her lips. "I mean, it's not over. Nothing's over until the fat lady sings. And in this case, that fat lady is me and you know how I feel about singing in public."

Olivia's laughter was dry and false. "I know."

"We're going to keep trying. If not with this fundraiser, then another," Amelia continued. "The Hesson House will rise again. You can mark my words."

But Olivia wasn't sure about that. In some ways, she had begun to let the concept of The Hesson House go. It had been a remarkable, albeit very brief, chapter in her life. She leaned her head against Anthony's chest as the feeling of loss washed over her. His hands clasped over her stomach as he swayed them both, to and fro. Perhaps it was over. Perhaps it was all truly over.

But as one of the last items arrived at the auction stage, Olivia noticed a shift in the mood. The item wasn't anything truly spectacular — just a light blue wardrobe with ornate detail along the edges. But a woman off to the right of the crowd had gotten the price up to forty-thousand dollars. Another man a few seats away had created a bidding war with her. Conversation halted around them as all eyes peered toward the two.

Finally, the light blue wardrobe sold to the woman for one-hundred thousand dollars. Olivia's eyes grew wide like saucers.

"What the heck was that?"

But the same story played out with the next item and then the next. Slowly, Olivia began to realize that she recognized the woman.

It was Great Aunt Marcia's granddaughter — a woman Olivia had been in a heated war with earlier in the year regarding The Hesson House itself. Marnie. Olivia hadn't seen her since she'd given Marnie the diaries and notes she had discovered in the basement of The Hesson House — diaries and notes Marnie had hoped were some sorts of treasure, which she had long since heard had been hidden in The Hesson House itself. Her disappointment had been palpable. And in the wake of it all, Olivia had been allowed to keep The Hesson House to herself.

It was remarkable to see her again.

Yet why was she there? And what was she after?

Olivia certainly knew better than to trust her.

When the auction was finalized, Marnie had ultimately spent upwards of two-hundred thousand dollars on four items. It was remarkable. Olivia stepped away from Anthony and hustled toward the woman, her mouth wide open with shock. She weaved through the oncoming traffic of people as they headed away from the auction, off to find wine and food. Marnie held back in conversation with that developer boyfriend of hers. PTSD from the previous February made Olivia shiver.

She appeared before Marnie, her brow furrowed. Marnie's beautiful eyes found hers. After a moment of silence, she said, in that sing-song voice of hers, "Oh. Hello, Olivia."

"What are you doing here?"

Despite her best intentions, Marnie couldn't very well not

sound like a mean-spirited woman. She exhaled as she stood to her full height, a few inches taller than Olivia.

"I read about your plight in the paper," she started to explain. "And I could not miss your little, quaint festival."

Olivia arched an eyebrow.

"But I couldn't help but feel that the funds weren't quite up to snuff to get The Hesson House back in order," Marnie continued. "So, myself and my partner over there — we boosted some of the prices." She winked at the man she had been in the bidding war with, who waved his little number toward her mischievously.

Olivia staggered back. "But why would you do that?"

Marnie sighed and stepped away from her boyfriend. She gestured for Olivia to keep up with her as she clicked her heels toward the far table, where she was meant to make arrangements for the movement of her goods.

"To be honest with you, Olivia, it's been a whirlwind of a year. After you gave me those items in that silly chest, I had a good think about my past, about the people in my life, about what really matters to me. And I realized that actually, I really did miss Grandma Marcia. She was a remarkable woman. She really was. And I treated everything and everyone she loved terribly in the wake of her death."

Amelia sat off to the side of the auction table. She scribbled notes to herself furiously. When she heard Olivia's voice, as Olivia tried and failed to stutter through some sort of response, she lifted her chin and then shook her head sadly.

"Still no?" Olivia asked.

"We're close, but no cigar."

Marnie's laughter twinkled. "Darling, you really should have called me. I can make up the difference. Don't you worry yourself."

Olivia wasn't entirely sure she wanted that. She swallowed the lump in her throat and tried to weigh her options. Marnie? Marnie hadn't had a single good bone in her body until recently. Could she really trust her?

"Don't worry yourself," Marnie continued. "I don't want to take over The Hesson House any longer. Perhaps it would be interesting to be listed as a partial owner? But I'm not married to the idea. Really, I just want to ensure that my grandmother's dream for that place can continue to flourish. I read every article written about the place over the summer. You created a perfect ecosystem—a beautiful space. I really must come around next summer, when you're back open. I hope you'll reserve the best suite for me."

Olivia shook her head delicately. "That's all you want?" They were foolish words, but she had to know.

Marnie nodded. "For the first time in my life, I can't think of another thing I want. Isn't that remarkable? Perhaps I'm going dull in my old age." Then, she delivered a beautiful smile, one that seemed almost real, almost believable. She then turned back toward the auctioneer to arrange for everything to be sent to the city.

Olivia walked like a zombie back toward Anthony.

"What happened? What did she say?" Anthony looked like an attack dog, hungry to protect.

"She wants to help," Olivia said, at a loss. "She wants to help us reopen. And she doesn't want anything in return."

Olivia fell against her fiancé after that. Her knees clacked together as he eased his hand down her back and whispered, "It's all going to be all right." Olivia had built up a boundary around herself and all her greatest desires. She'd never envisioned that she would fall in love again; she had never envisioned The Hesson House would have the space and the funds to reopen. But here they were — on the brink of winter, on the verge of the rest of their lives. And she was completely and totally content.

CHAPTER TWENTY-THREE

THE WAIT WAS TOO UNBEARABLE. It left Olivia shivering with excitement. Against Anthony's advice to let it go till Monday, Olivia called the contractor the following morning and told him with a burst of excitement that they would be able to break ground on the rebuild and refurbishing on The Hesson House as soon as possible. He suggested that they meet at the site later that afternoon for another analysis.

"I'm so happy to hear that," he said. "Really. It's a beautiful space. It deserves to flourish."

Olivia, Anthony, Xavier, and Chelsea piled into Olivia's car and sped out to The Hesson House. That drive had once been so familiar, and now, Olivia relished every second of it. The sunlight caught the diamond of her ring and reflected out beautifully, so much so that Chelsea complained that the light might blind her.

"Good," Anthony said. "I told the woman at the jewelry store that I wanted the kind of diamond that could blind someone, so it could be used as a weapon."

"When am I going to need to use my ring as a weapon?" Olivia asked, laughing.

"I don't know. It could come in handy, though," Anthony joked. "Like now, when you want to annoy your daughter."

"Good point," Olivia said as she flashed her daughter again with that bright light.

"You guys are gross," Chelsea offered, even as her smile remained plastered between her ears.

Up at The Hesson House, the contractor led them again through the foyer, around the grounds, past the tennis court, toward the now-dilapidated boathouse. He made notes, asked questions, and then stated that if all went according to plan, they could have The Hesson House back up and running by April or May. Olivia clutched Anthony's hand excitedly. They would be given a whole summer to try again.

A celebration was in order. Olivia texted her best friends and her family members and announced that they would have a dinner and a bonfire up on The Hesson House grounds, with a start time at three.

MILA: Seriously? Isabelle and Zane are both home! We'd love to come!

CAMILLA: What should we bring?

AMELIA: Cool if I bring Mandy? We had plans today.

Olivia's text messages rang out after that — that everyone was invited, of course; that wine and more wine was always welcome; that they'd probably have hot dogs and hamburgers and anything else grill-worthy for this particularly glorious day in early October.

JENNIFER: I'll bring tons of desserts!

Her mother, father, brother, and his family also agreed to the barbecue. When Olivia invited Marnie, however, she sent only this:

MARNIE: You know I don't eat barbecue.

MARNIE: You'll receive the funds this week.

MARNIE: Ciao.

Firewood was needed for the upcoming gathering. Olivia and Chelsea set out through the woods to gather what they could. As they walked quietly, Olivia removed her engagement ring again and held it up, examining it.

"He did good," Chelsea affirmed then, her first words to her mother in quite some time.

"He really did, didn't he?" Olivia returned her gaze to Chelsea. Again, she felt it: that strange tension between them. How could they force themselves through it? "I hope you know you'll have to be another maid of honor."

"I'm in high demand these days, I guess," Chelsea returned with a grin.

Olivia laughed tenderly. Her heart ached to ask Chelsea everything that had happened since her arrival back to the island a few weeks before. She yearned for the kind of mother-daughter relationship that lacked boundaries. Perhaps that was never really possible. Even on Gilmore Girls, Lorelei and Rory had grappled with that sometimes.

"Dad came back to the city," Chelsea suddenly said. "To say he was sorry. And tell me the baby was born."

Olivia's heart jumped into her throat. This was it—the truth.

Chelsea drew a line with her finger across the bark of the nearest tree. She simply couldn't look into Olivia's eyes as she explained.

"He's started therapy and AA. And he seems better, although I know I shouldn't completely trust in him yet," Chelsea told her. She huffed and then added, "I don't know what it is about Dad. I guess just trauma from the past. I never really got over his leaving. And when he wants me in his life, I freak out. I need to handle that better. Really look at it for what it is."

"He's just lost and being somewhat immature about the whole thing. Like all of us act sometimes but him more so than most," Olivia said tenderly.

"I guess that's true. We all have our moments," Chelsea agreed.

Olivia placed her hand on Chelsea's shoulder and massaged it gently. "Everything okay between you and Xav?"

"Yes. Now that Dad's gone and we've been allowed to really start our new life, everything is great."

"I knew you could handle it— all of it. You're only nineteen, but you have the bravery of a much older woman," Olivia said.

"Thanks for saying that. It really means a lot."

Olivia bowed her head. Silence passed between them.

"I don't think I want to be a teacher anymore," Olivia said suddenly.

Chelsea's eyebrows rose. "Really!"

"Yeah. I think this might be my last year." Olivia hadn't known the power of this emotion until now, as she spoke it aloud to her daughter. "I want to throw myself completely into The Hesson House. And I've been writing. Silly stuff, maybe — but I also might want to write a book about Great Aunt Marcia."

Chelsea's smile erupted. "That's incredible, Mom."

"Thank you for saying that."

"Too bad it's only October. You have many more months of teaching," Chelsea said.

"True. But it'll be good to close out the year with them," Olivia said. "Really give it my all until The Hesson House reopens."

"Are you going to finally let the kids read what they've always wanted to read? Books about sex and drugs and rock 'n roll?" Chelsea asked.

"Not quite. I want to give my notice, not get fired," Olivia clarified.

The bonfire crackled and spat and threatened to tear itself toward the sky. Olivia and Chelsea piled their new firewood off to the side; the fire would eat it when it was ready.

"I'm just glad it's not still wet from the storm," Anthony said. "That could have been a real problem."

"Funny that all this space was just ocean a few weeks ago," Olivia pointed out as she kicked the ground.

"And a restaurant before that," Anthony affirmed.

"Now, it's just a bonfire," Olivia breathed.

"But it has space and time to be anything else," Anthony said. "We just have to will it to existence."

Jennifer, Derek, Nick, his fiancé, Stacy, Camilla, Jonathon, Andrea, Isaac, Mila, Liam, Isabelle, Zane, Amelia, Mandy, and Oliver, arrived a few minutes after three — all of them touting bottles of wine, bags of chips, hot dogs, hamburger meat, freshly-cut vegetables, fruits, and desserts galore. In their wake, Olivia's parents, her brother Jared, along with his family, arrived. Some of the guys carried a few of the left-over plastic tables out from the basement and lined them across the grounds, while Anthony started up the grill they'd brought down from the hotel itself. As he heated the charcoal, he whistled to himself. Olivia wrapped her arms around his sturdy frame and inhaled his scent — sandalwood and sage and something else, something uniquely his. For the zillionth time in twenty-four hours, her mother grabbed her hand and inspected the ring, then spoke at length about Olivia's options for wedding gowns.

"I think Mom should wear whatever she wants," Chelsea pointed out as she sat on a log near the fire.

"Yes, but within reason," her mother countered.

"Yes. When Mom told me she wanted to wear a toga down the aisle, I wasn't so sure about it," Chelsea said.

"A toga?" Her mother looked stricken.

"Chelsea is pulling your leg, Mom," Olivia laughed. "Chelsea, can you try to control yourself for like, five minutes?"

"No can do, Mom," Chelsea returned. She then placed her head on Xavier's shoulder and winked.

But this, of course, led her grandmother to dig into her with countless questions. "How is it in the city? Have you seen any crimes? What is your apartment like? Is it true that every apartment in New York City is infested with cockroaches?"

"It's true," Andrea confirmed as she joined in. "You can count on me to tell the truth."

"Chelsea! You absolutely must move home," her grandmother spouted.

"She's just pulling your leg, Grandma," Chelsea chuckled at her grandmother. She was so gullible. "Me and Xavier have an okay place. It's not Buckingham Palace, but it keeps us warm at night."

"Do you think you'll do anything different with the hotel now that you have to redo it?" her father asked as he appeared beside her, beer in hand.

Olivia gazed up at the beautiful mansion; the old stones glistened beneath the October sun, and the bright red, yellow, and orange leaves made the view a gorgeous streak of vibrant colors.

"I don't think so. Do you have any recommendations?"

Her father considered this. "I think you should have a sauna."

"Huh. Actually, not a bad idea," Olivia said. "Very sellable in the pamphlets."

"Exactly my thought," he returned. "And you know, I can help out with anything you need. It's going to be a hard road. I'm sure you feel like you're back to square one."

"Not really, surprisingly," Olivia told him. "Yes, the hotel is about as ready to open as it was last February when I inherited it. But along the way, I've gained so much. A fiancé, for example, and a huge sense of purpose. I can't explain it, but it really feels like everything that happened was for a reason. Doesn't that sound so silly?"

"It doesn't," her father told her. "I've thought that so many times over the years, especially when I look around at your mom, your sister, your brother and my grandkids. I can't believe every decision led me to this point. But it must have."

"It must have," Olivia echoed.

Anthony and Olivia portioned out the hot dogs and hamburgers on various plates. Chelsea had chopped lettuce and tomato and onion, which she portioned out on several large plates, to allow for all the guests to pass through and decorate their own burger and hot dog to their hearts' content. Perhaps in previous years, Chelsea might have grumbled at the idea of helping out; now, however, she flung herself into action — becoming a part of the great cycle of women in their family. Kim and Olivia and Chelsea — and someday, maybe, Chelsea's daughter; they would all find one another in the kitchen at various holidays, gossiping and ensuring everyone else was fed.

Toward the far log, Chelsea and Andrea fell into another conversation about Andrea's approaching wedding. Camilla collapsed on the picnic table alongside Olivia and said, "Wedding, wedding, wedding. Will it ever end?"

"I don't think you want it to," Olivia told her.

Camilla smiled playfully. "You're right. I don't. I'll soak up every minute."

"And when do you think yours will be?" Jennifer asked.

Olivia turned her gaze back to meet Anthony's. "I don't think there's any rush. After all, we'll want to have it here, after everything's finished. Don't you think, Tony?"

Anthony laughed. "I told her I hated when my dad called my Tony, and now, she's picked up on it."

"You're evil, Olivia Hesson," Mila quipped.

"Maybe a little bit," Olivia returned.

"I had to get it from somewhere," Chelsea said.

"A wedding at The Hesson House? What a dream that will be," Amelia breathed.

"And what about you?" Kim demanded of Amelia.

"What about me, what?" Amelia asked, her burger poised.

"You know." Kim wagged her eyebrows.

"She's suggesting you should get married before you have a

baby," Olivia said with a funny grin. "But you shouldn't listen to her."

Amelia shrugged lightly and laughed it off. "If you'd told me ten years ago about the way everything worked out, I would have told you that you were crazy. But life is funny that way. Right, Oliver?"

Oliver beamed and dotted a kiss on her cheek. "And thank goodness for that," he added.

The fire continued to spit and crackle into the evening. Olivia's nearest and dearest bubbled with life and conversation. Everyone spoke over everyone else — with Olivia's mother the most frequent offender. Olivia laughed so hard that her stomach ached. And through it all, Anthony sat beside her, his hand gently on her knee — her knight in shining armor, her rock through it all. Soon, winter would come; the leaves would die and flutter to the ground. Martha's Vineyard would burrow itself beneath layers of snow and when spring came, The Hesson House would rise again — better and stronger than ever.

Like Olivia herself.

The Vineyard Sunset Series

Secrets of Mackinac Island Series

Sisters of Edgartown Series

A Katama Bay Series